"What are
to do

Brad stared   efore he
replied. "Th   said evenly, "is
entirely up to you, Julie. Your stepfather
has stolen five thousand pounds."

"Five thousand!" Julie croaked. "Then
why did he go to you? You're the boss;
why did he expect you to help him? Stop
playing with me, Brad! When will you
call the police?"

"I can prevent police involvement," he
drawled slowly, "but only with the right
encouragement I want you to live
with me."

"You asked me before," she gasped,
meaning that he was wasting his time.

"I'm asking you again, for the last time."
Cold challenge rang in his voice. "Agree,
and I'll put back every penny your
stepfather stole. If not, then I'm afraid
there's nothing I can do."

Dark Surrender

by

MARGARET PARGETER

Harlequin Books

TORONTO • LONDON • LOS ANGELES • AMSTERDAM
SYDNEY • HAMBURG • PARIS • STOCKHOLM • ATHENS • TOKYO

Original hardcover edition published in 1980
by Mills & Boon Limited

ISBN 0-373-02409-6

Harlequin edition published June 1981

Printed in U.S.A.

CHAPTER ONE

'CALL for you, Miss Gray. Mr Hewson's office.'

Aware that the supervisor of the typing pool was doing her best to hide her annoyance, Julie hurried over to the telephone. As she left her desk she stumbled, so that when she spoke it was in a husky whisper. 'Julie Gray here.'

'Julie? Can't you speak up? I can't hear you.' Brad Hewson's voice came over so loudly that Julie knew Miss Harrison, who hovered fretfully, must have overheard.

'It—it's not very convenient, Brad,' she protested feebly. 'We're busy.' In spite of any kudos it might bring, she wished Brad hadn't taken to ringing her during office hours. For one thing, she would rather have kept quiet about her friendship with the head of the firm, as it could never last. Not like this, anyway. 'I'm very busy!' she repeated, more firmly.

'I hope you are,' his voice still held a mixture of amusement and impatience. 'I won't keep you. I've just realised that I have nothing much on this afternoon and could pick you up about five.'

'But, Brad,' she cried, with rising agitation, 'I don't finish at five!'

'Make sure you do today, sweetheart.'

The line went dead. Julie dropped the receiver as if it were red hot. She was aware that many of the girls whom she worked with had been listening with unashamed curiosity, half green with envy, but this was no comfort. Brad might be the boss, and Hewson's was quite a giant in the private car industry, but this was all the more reason why he should realise she couldn't ask for time off which she wasn't entitled to, even if it was only half an hour.

'Is something worrying you, Julie?' Miss Harrison asked smoothly.

Julie started, suddenly conscious of everyone looking at her. Her cheeks going pink, she again blessed Brad Hewson's arrogance as she stammered reluctantly. 'I'm not worrying exactly, Miss Harrison, but—er—Mr Hewson would like me to meet him at five.'

Miss Harrison frowned. 'I wish Mr Hewson would try to remember that if I grant one of my staff favours everyone will want them.'

'I did try to tell him.' Miss Harrison's procedure in this particular instance was growing familiar, and Julie was beginning to hate it.

'What shall I do, girls?' With an unusually indulgent smile, Miss Harrison glanced around the office, well aware that everyone was closely interested in the romance which was apparently blossoming between Brad Hewson and a member of his staff. Some might be less kind in their remarks than others, but they were all interested.

In spite of Julie's obvious embarrassment, they all laughed, and their reply was almost unanimous. 'Let her go, Miss Harrison. Providing she tells us all about it in the morning.' Someone added, 'If I had your looks, young Julie, I wouldn't hesitate!'

Feeling worse than ever, Julie retreated back to her desk. Her fellow workers were, on the whole, a generous lot. There were one or two who remained silent, though, making her uncomfortably aware that not everyone wished her well. And it was rumoured that Norma Jenkins, up in management, who had chased Brad Hewson for years, was far from pleased at this new development. Wryly Julie recognised that her friendship with Brad had little chance of passing unnoticed. It might have been different if he had just been one of the men on the assembly line.

At five she left the office as unobtrusively as possible, a tallish, slender girl of twenty-one, supple and graceful with an elegance she didn't know she possessed. Her hair was tawny in colour, and she wore it straight and long. It swung out behind her now, shining beautifully in the last rays of afternoon sunshine, as she ran down to the corner where Brad usually picked her up.

His car was there, waiting. It always brought a warm glow to her heart that he never kept her hanging about. He saw her coming and a smile creased his dark, rugged face as he leaned over and swung the door open. When she got in he leaned over again, closing it behind her, making her feeling cosseted.

'All right?' Before straightening he turned his head to look at her, kissing her mouth lightly, something he did very well. He had dropped her off that morning, and spoken to her over the telephone since, but he made it seem as though he hadn't seen her in weeks.

A practised philanderer? As she smiled back at him, answering casually, the thought flashed mockingly through Julie's head.

He glanced at her narrowly, almost as if he had guessed what she was thinking, but he only said briefly, 'Fasten your seat belt, there's a good girl.'

While he steered the low, powerful car through the side streets to join the main stream of traffic, Julie's blue eyes flickered to his strong, handsome profile. For the first time she found herself nervous of his straight, decisive nose, the deeply cleft chin, the strong, determined jawline. She would be a naïve little fool to believe that a man of thirty-six, who was as good-looking as Brad Hewson, was without experience when it came to women. Yet he had never asked her to have an affair with him, and he had been taking her out, off and on, for several weeks now. Their relationship, so far, had been casual, but they had become good friends. This, she had decided, without stopping to analyse it, was perhaps what Brad needed—all he was looking for, a good friend.

Joe, Julie's stepfather, had suggested teasingly that Brad could have marriage in mind, a remark which she had instantly dismissed. The notion, however, must have stuck, as she found herself dwelling on it occasionally. For several reasons Julie discovered the idea of being married to Brad was not displeasing, bringing with it as it did a hint of respectability. Not that she was over-concerned about that, but, judging from what the girls said in the office, she must be fortunate to know a man whose sole aim wasn't to get a girl to bed as quickly as possible. While something instinctively told her that Brad might eventually want something more than a few light kisses, she felt that whatever the future held it couldn't be bad. She couldn't be continually worrying about what was to follow, and for the present she was content.

As they left the city of Derby behind she roused herself. 'Where are we going, Brad?'

'Home,' he replied briefly.

Astonished, she sat up. 'You don't mean to say you asked me to get out early just to go home?'

'Why not?' His mouth quirked lazily at her young indignation. 'Don't you like going home with me, Julie?'

'You know that's not what I mean,' she said sharply. 'I don't mind asking for time off if it's for something special. I'll have to make it up ...'

'No, you won't,' he said curtly. Then, dryly, 'If the company loses money through your taking a few minutes off, I promise to stand the loss myself.'

'All the same, I wish you wouldn't. If everyone left early you wouldn't be so complacent.'

Ignoring what she said, he asked abruptly, 'Didn't I see you talking to young Rodney Green during your lunch hour?'

'Rodney? Oh, yes.' She had almost forgotten. She hadn't noticed Brad and wondered where he had been.

'You appeared to have a lot to discuss?'

She tried hard to remember. 'I don't think it was anything important. His firework party, I believe. Rodney likes to talk and we've know each other a long time.'

Brad Hewson slanted her a quick, thoughtful glance. 'I suppose that's true, as you both live in the same village. Did he offer you a lift home, too?'

He had, but Julie didn't say so. Something in Brad's tone made her skin suddenly prickle, in a way she couldn't remember happening before. It seemed to warn her to go carefully, as did the tight angle of his jaw. Evasively she replied, 'He knows that, lately anyway, I've been going home with you.'

'Good.' Brad put his hand out to take hers lightly before pressing his foot to the floorboards. As the car leapt forward, he said with some satisfaction, 'We should be back in ten minutes. I was going to ask you to have tea with me.'

'I didn't know you bothered with anything so mundane,' she laughed, relaxing again as he let go of her hand. She wasn't sure how she felt when he touched her. There was plenty of sensation, but she couldn't decide if it was pleasant. It was pleasant to know, though, that he didn't intend dropping her off on her own doorstep, as he passed it.

'Only when I have someone as lovely as you to share it with,' he teased softly, putting an arm around her shoulders to draw her gently to him. 'Today, somehow, I find the idea of hot tea and buttered crumpets in front of the fire most tempting.'

'Oh, you do, do you!' Hiding a quick grin, she pretended to feel affronted and pulled away from him. Switching on the radio without asking permission, she lay back in the comfortable leather seat, her chin lifted haughtily in the air.

Again Brad laughed softly, then gave his attention to the road. All he said, in a low, threatening kind of voice, was, 'Yes!'

Letting him concentrate on his driving, Julie considered how nice it would be to share Brad's tea. It was October, the nights were pulling in and getting colder, but it was cosy in Brad's study when the curtains were drawn and the flames in the great fireplace were leaping halfway up the chimney. If Brad was in a good mood he might allow her to play some of his records. He always had some she liked. This was another thing they shared, a similar taste in music. Joe wouldn't be home until seven, so there was no hurry.

Joe was Julie's stepfather. After her mother died she had continued to live with him in the small rented cottage at the end of the village. Their house was about a mile from Brad's.

It was strange, Julie mused, how history had a way of almost repeating itself. A few years ago her mother had told her how she and Brad's father had fallen in love, before World War Two. Brad's grandparents had unfortunately been horrified. They could never allow their only son to marry the daughter of an ordinary working man. They had taken him away to another house which they owned on the south coast, where he had apparently soon got over his foolish infatuation. Within a year or two he had married and Brad had been born. While it had taken Julie's mother much longer to recover, she had, in fact, married twice.

The war had come and Hewsons had made a lot of money from building tanks and other vehicles, but they had never returned to the village. The house stood empty until about a year ago when Bradley Hewson, Henry's son, arrived, and began putting it right. He had had to practically rebuild it, but Julie knew he considered it had been worth all the time and expense he had lavished on it. Now it was a beautiful place, a home of which to be proud.

Brad had been too busy to get to know many of the local people. If it hadn't been for Joe, Julie might never have made his acquaintance. Joe, who was well up in management at Hewsons, had got Julie a job there, after she left secretarial college. Each day they travelled to work in Joe's small car, but one morning, when it broke down and refused to start, they had been forced to run for a bus.

This was when Julie had first met Brad Hewson. He had seen them running, Julie's tawny hair flying, her blue eyes sparkling, her cheeks flushed. Pulling up, he asked Joe if they would like a lift, but it was at Julie he had looked. Reed-slim, full of young, healthy vitality, she stood beside Joe, her breath coming quickly. She wasn't really beautiful, but she had a fine clear skin and wide, dark blue eyes which always attracted a lot of attention. She hadn't realised, as she did her share of staring, how her slightly parted lips were like an invitation. It was only when Brad's glance slid contemplatively to the shapely curves of her graceful figure that she flinched uneasily and slipped self-consciously into the coat she was carrying. The mockery in his eyes had clashed head on with the resentment in her own as she had done so.

That morning it had only been for Joe's sake that she accepted that lift, as Joe had managed to whisper that it was the boss and she hadn't wanted to offend him. Almost diving to the back seat of the kind of car she had never thought to ride in, she had sat in cold silence until they reached Derby. Her vision unavoidably filled with a close view of Brad Hewson's broad shoulders, the dark lines of his handsome profile, before leaving him she thanked him with a cool politeness which had merely appeared to amuse him.

After that morning, because Joe's car had been a write-off and he couldn't afford another, Brad Hewson often picked them up. He soon dealt with Julie's wavering anti-pathy, and though she realised he set out to do this deliber-ately, she also suspected that very few women would be able to resist him when he chose to be pleasant. He had, she secretly admitted, more than his fair share of charm.

He intended living here, he told them. He kept a flat in London, which was useful, but he was going to make Haydon Hill his permanent home.

'Maybe he intends getting married?' Joe had pondered thoughtfully over his supper. 'Though the talk goes that he likes his pleasure too much to settle down.'

'Perhaps he hasn't met the right woman,' Julie retorted hollowly. The thought of Brad Hewson bringing a bride to the village had made her feel suddenly miserable, although she couldn't have said why.

'Perhaps not,' Joe shrugged.

A week or two later, Brad had asked Julie to have dinner with him. He suggested it so casually that Julie's growing wariness had temporarily faded. He waylaid her in the works canteen, a place she was sure he didn't normally frequent. She had been startled to find him blocking her path and even more so by his invitation.

'If you've nothing better to do this evening, Julie, will you come and have a meal with me?' His mouth had quirked as she hesitated. 'I promise not to keep you out too late.'

Instinctively cautious, Julie had been about to refuse, but so many faces were turned towards them that she found herself accepting with an almost indelicate haste. Anything to be rid of him! He had looked more than capable of arguing about it, regardless of an interested audience.

'Thank you, Mr Hewson,' she said loudly. 'Will that be all?'

Which ought to have convinced those who were straining their ears that they were only discussing business! She wasn't sure what kind of business Brad could be expected to be discussing with a girl like herself, but she hadn't stopped to think. Probably she knew if she did she would only feel incredibly foolish. As it was, she had been sure he'd been laughing at her, even as he replied soberly, 'Yes, Miss Gray, that will be all, for the moment.'

Since then there had been many such outings, but not once had Brad done anything more serious than place a light goodnight kiss on her cheek. It was as if he sensed how young she was, despite her twenty or more years, and wanted to do nothing to cause her disquiet. Regarding her own feelings, Julie couldn't make up her mind. She refused to think of Brad Hewson as anything other than a friend, yet she found he could make her pulse race in a most frightening way. This couldn't be because she was falling in love with him. If anything, in those early days, she had felt quite the reverse. Sometimes she was sure the strong emotion which stirred in her heart was hate. Hatred for all the misery his family had caused her mother, and she knew an urgent desire to make him suffer. But since Brad, like herself, hadn't been born then, and the people concerned were no longer alive, it seemed a slightly ridiculous path to pursue. There didn't seem much point in revenge any more.

'Here we are.' Brad drew up in front of the house, laughing at Julie's startled face. 'What were you dreaming about, or shouldn't I ask?'

'You,' she exclaimed, without thinking. Quickly pulling herself together, she smiled ruefully, 'It wasn't all nice, so don't ask me to be more explicit.'

His eyes gleaming sardonically, he caught her hand, jerking her to him. Bending his head, he kissed her surprised mouth. As she drew back sharply, he frowned. 'I meant to punish you, but not all that much. What's wrong?'

'Why, nothing, I suppose.' Beneath his sceptical glance she felt a sudden rush of warmth to her cheeks. 'It's just —well, that's the second time in less than an hour, and anyone could have seen us.' When his expression changed to one of mocking amusement, she added fiercely, 'I'm not as used to kissing in public as you obviously are!'

'I've certainly never believed in restraining myself on my own doorstep,' he taunted, 'especially when there's no one around. Two chaste kisses in an hour doesn't constitute rape, you know. Why don't you grow up a little, Julie?'

'I am grown up.'

'Then learn to relax. Most women enjoy this kind of thing. When I'm in the right mood,' he grinned, 'I even enjoy it myself, and you must admit I've been very patient so far.'

So he was lumping her with all the other women he knew? No doubt he knew many very permissive ones! He was very physical himself. Shaken by such a thought, and rather ashamed, as he had never yet stepped out of line with her, Julie murmured, 'I'm sorry, Brad. Sometimes I wonder why you bother with me.'

'Do you?' He sat for a moment, considering this, his eyes on her closely, then he smiled again. 'Come on, let's go in. If you're good I might tell you while we're having tea.'

Inside, he ordered his manservant to bring tea and toast, and some cakes if he could find any, to the study. After relieving Julie of her jacket, he told her to make herself at home while he changed into something less formal than his office suit. He wouldn't be many minutes.

The central heating was on, but this didn't prevent Julie from crouching beside the fire, holding her hands out to the welcoming blaze. She wished she had been able to change to something lighter herself. Office skirts were not notoriously glamorous. She might have asked Brad to stop as they had passed the cottage, but she sensed, somehow, that he had no particular liking for the plain little house.

The telephone rang. She waited, not sure what to do as neither Brad nor his manservant came to answer, but at last she nerved herself to lift the receiver. It was probably not her place, and Brad might tell her so—there again, he might be annoyed if she just left it.

'Haydon Hill,' she said politely.

'Oh!' The sweetly feminine voice sounded startled. There was a slight pause before the lady asked, 'Is Mr Hewson in? I've tried the works, but he's not there.'

'Yes. He's upstairs, as a matter of fact.'

'I see.' Another pause. 'To whom am I speaking?'

'I—I work for him.'

'Ah ...' the tone changed to a kind of relieved impatience. 'Then for goodness' sake, girl, isn't there an extension?'

'Yes.'

'Well, put me straight through to Mr Hewson!'

Julie obliged, waiting until Brad spoke before putting down her receiver. As she went back to the fire, her renewed contemplation of the flames held little pleasure. Whoever the woman was she sounded smart and intelligent, and as if she knew Brad very well. Julie felt a pang of curiosity along with a surprising quiver of pain.

Foster, the manservant, appeared with their tea moments before Brad arrived. A thrill of relief coursed through Julie's veins at the sight of him, as though she had been frightened his mysterious caller had taken him away. He was wearing beige slacks, belted to his supple waist, and a checked, toning shirt. His dark hair was thick and waved but always looked well groomed, and his smile was full of a warm charm as he came over and took her hands. Again she felt the warning flickers which she experienced whenever he touched her. A strange response which she tried desperately to hide.

'Thanks for putting Viola through,' he didn't attempt to ignore the subject. 'I'm having dinner with her tomorrow evening.'

Returning his smile, Julie wondered why her face felt so stiff. 'I believe she thinks I work here.'

'I shouldn't be surprised.' Squeezing her hands gently, he let go of them to pour himself a drink. 'Viola always jumps to the conclusion that suits her best.' Idly he paused. 'Are you going to join me?'

'Oh, no!' Julie cried, only just realising what he was doing. 'You asked me to tea, but I won't enjoy it if you aren't having some too.'

He stood watching her with narrowed eyes before putting down his whisky with a sigh. 'You sound exactly like a nagging wife,' he teased softly.

'Is that why you've never married?' she countered, a crazy weakness in her stomach. 'To escape the nagging?'

'Partly,' he smiled, his eyes crinkling as they met her uncertain ones. 'I've always believed that life can hold much more fun for those who remain single. Which doesn't necessarily mean alone.'

'For men, perhaps.' She flushed but tried to match his frankness.

'Why not for women, too?'

She knew he noticed the cup she passed him wobbled slightly. 'We don't have exactly the same kind of freedom, do we?'

He looked amused. 'Why don't you call a spade a spade, Julie? You're talking of sexual freedom, of course?'

'I—I suppose so.' Brad had indicated she should pour, but she wasn't making a very good job of it! Some of her tea slopped over and she had to wipe it up. Vaguely she hoped it wouldn't mark the table. 'It's different for women,' she murmured, when he told her to stop fussing.

'Many women wouldn't agree with you.' His glance was suddenly keener than Julie thought the subject warranted. 'They enjoy their new liberation and, personally, I think it's a good thing. It certainly can save a lot of bother.'

'I'm afraid I ...' she paused, feeling out of her depth, aware of undercurrents she was maybe too young to interpret. Strangely shaken, she managed a careless shrug. 'Does it really matter? I merely meant that men don't run the same risks.'

'When they have an affair, you mean?' his dark brows rose humorously. 'I suppose it depends how involved they are. Mostly I've found women well able to look after themselves.'

Gazing at him blankly, Julie found it incredible that they were having such a conversation. A slight feather of steam rose from her teacup; her eyes flickered to it blankly before she looked at Brad again. 'I'm sure you will be right about some, but like everything else you can't generalise,' she retorted.

He stared searchingly into her eyes. 'That sounds as if it should tell me something,' he probed coolly. 'Haven't you ever been deeply involved with a man, Julie?'

Feeling suddenly defeated, she made a great effort to drag her eyes from the sombre insistence of his. Was he about to suggest they go away for a weekend? Was this what all this was leading up to? Shouldn't she have seen it coming? 'I don't go in for that sort of thing,' she replied, with a very young dignity.

'Not even occasionally?' he persisted dryly.

'No!' Her soft mouth quivered as she continued recklessly, 'And I think I know what you're getting at!'

Allowing a moment's silence to elapse, he said gently, 'Your eyes are beautiful, Julie, especially when you're alarmed about something, but you don't have to be worried. I don't want you to feel you're in any danger.'

Immediately she was ashamed. Tension drained from her as he placed a reassuring hand over her own. 'I'm sorry, Brad. I'm not really frightened of you. It's just that I believe in certain things.'

'I know,' his mood swung to harsh irony, 'you're saving yourself for a man who can afford to pay for all your highly held principles? What else will he get, I wonder? Package deals are all the rage, but I believe many turn out to be somewhat disappointing.'

Carefully Julie put down her cup and saucer, knowing instinctively she was suddenly treading on dangerous ground. Brad's face had hardened, the dark grey eyes becoming those of a stranger, and his hard but sensuous mouth had gone oddly taut. The conversation had affected her too. Her heart beat faster and her legs felt curiously weak. 'I'd better go now, Brad,' she whispered, 'I have Joe's dinner to cook.'

For a second she thought he was going to be angry, but all he said was, 'Right. I'll run you back in five minutes. After you thank me properly for your tea.'

As she began to oblige with a small flurry of words, he startled her by reaching out and drawing her across his knee. 'What on earth do you think you're doing?' she heard herself faltering unsteadily.

He smiled down into her widening blue eyes, his physical attraction compelling. 'I should have thought that was perfectly obvious? Surely I deserve some kind of reward for all the restraint I practise, not to mention the lifts I give you to work?'

The faint smile on his mouth, the glint in his eye suggested he was teasing her again, but she didn't want to deny him anything. As she stared up at the vitally handsome face poised above hers, her heart still raced, but she felt happier. He recognised the restrictions she imposed, so perhaps she could afford to be generous. Closing her eyes against the deep penetration of his, she slid her arms experimentally around his shoulders.

Brad didn't assault her ferociously, as she had half expected. Instead he kissed her mouth gently before going on to explore her cheeks and the soft hollows of her neck, his arms only tightening gradually. Eventually he came back to her mouth, finding at last the response he sought so assiduously. One arm held her taut body to him while the other soothed her back, lingering on the warm curve of her waist, hesitating, then staying where it was.

Moments passed, her breath becoming more difficult to find. Sparks were striking her now from Brad's ruthless mouth and the probing persuasiveness of his hands. A fiery glow spread through her as inexorably he drew her closer. She felt drugged while fully aware of his dangerous power. Her body went oddly still, waiting.

Then the telephone rang; someone was also ringing the doorbell. There were voices in the hall and suddenly she was sitting on the sofa by herself. Blindly she reached for her coat as Brad dealt abruptly with the telephone. When, with a curt word of apology, he left the room, she dragged herself to her feet and followed.

In the hall she found him talking to a woman. Without stopping to be introduced Julie walked straight past them, a fixed smile on her disturbed face. She wasn't sure what she felt. If anything it was gratitude that someone had called at this particular hour.

Brad spoke sharply. 'If you'll wait, Julie, I'll run you home in a few minutes.'

'Thanks, Brad,' she managed casually, avoiding his intent glance, 'but I think I'll just walk.'

'As you like,' he agreed, so coldly that she flinched.

'Goodbye, then,' she muttered, more uncertainly.

'I'll give you a ring,' he called after her.

Joe was in when she reached the cottage. Having failed, on her twenty-minute walk, to unravel the mystery of her own feelings, Julie rushed upstairs, unable to face Joe straight away. She felt too distraught, inclined to blame Brad resentfully, for thrusting on her a knowledge she would rather have been without. Until this afternoon she had at least had peace of mind. Now she wasn't sure what she had. Previously there had only been fleeting glimpses, gleaned mostly from other people's lives, of the tantalising, intimate pressures which could exist between a man and a woman. Now Brad had filled her with a kind of restless fever to know more than was permissible, for a girl who was trying to hang on to her principles!

Brad might be cruel, she thought, as she quickly washed her face and ran a comb through her tangled hair. He had looked quite unmoved, as she had left his house, yet his mouth on hers had been warm and exciting. As strange emotions invaded her, Julie knew she must be very careful when she was alone with him, after this. He might have deliberately set out to show her how vulnerable she was, how weak her arguments were, but whatever he had done to her—and she supposed he would consider a few kisses and caresses not much—it had shaken her to the very core of her being. Bitterly regretful that she couldn't just forget him, she went downstairs again, to get Joe his supper.

'No need to rush,' he smiled. 'Edith and I are going out for dinner. She's calling for me. It will save you bothering to cook.'

'Oh, I see,' Julie hesitated. Edith Kirby was a neighbour. She and Joe had become very friendly lately, but how could Joe afford to take her out when his bank balance was in the red and only that morning he had complained of being broke? Perhaps Edith was paying? She was a spinster and had a good job. Julie grimaced wryly. It wasn't really any of her business and Joe wouldn't thank her for interfering. She smiled at him. 'I hope you have a good evening.'

'We will.' Joe rubbed his hands together happily. 'Have you just got in, Julie?'

'Yes. I——' she swallowed nervously, 'that is, Brad brought me from town, but I had tea with him before coming back here.'

'I didn't hear a car.' Joe was inspecting the inner pocket of his jacket, making sure he had everything.

'You'd have been clever if you had,' she attempted to joke. 'I walked from Haydon.'

Joe frowned, his short figure suddenly stiff, his florid face increasing in colour, which Julie took for anger. 'You —walked?'

She was startled by Joe's reaction and said hastily, 'Someone called on him just as I was leaving. Brad did offer, but I thought it would be quicker if I walked. Maybe if I'd known you were going out I would have waited.'

'Oh, well, if that's all——' he began, as Edith tooted outside. 'I'd better go,' he laughed, his mood restored, as he went out.

Edith had a small car, in almost as bad a condition as Joe's had been, but like Joe she was too fond of extravagant foreign holidays to afford a new one. Julie wondered if Joe and Edith were serious about each other. They could easily be, she admitted. She had promised her mother she would look after Joe, but wasn't wholly convinced she'd be sorry to lose him. Joe had been her stepfather for over ten years, and she knew he was fond of her. He had legally adopted her and changed her name to his. About the latter Julie had some regrets, but she had been too young when it had happened to protest. As things had turned out, while they had always been good friends, they had never been very close. If Joe did marry again then she would have to get a room on her own somewhere. Edith was nice, but this cottage would be much too small for two women.

Glad of anything to take her mind off Brad, she considered whether it would be better to live in Derby or go to London. Probably London would be best and, as she was nearly twenty-two, it was maybe time she branched out on her own. In London there would be less chance of running into Brad, which might not be a bad thing as, after tonight, she felt uneasy about seeing him again.

Edith and Joe hadn't been gone more than fifteen minutes when Brad rang. 'You sound surprised,' he laughed. 'I said I would ring, but you were in such a tearing hurry. Surely I didn't scare you all that much?'

'I'm not sure ...' she spoke hoarsely, a curious tightness in her throat.

'You have the makings of a very permissive little witch, once you let yourself go,' he chuckled. When she didn't answer, he stopped laughing and said he was sorry. 'Even the line sounds disapproving. Will you have dinner with me, Julie, just to prove I'm forgiven?'

She was too bewildered, and too frightened of making the wrong decision to do anything else but agree. Yet, at the sound of his voice, her heart began pounding, and as she got ready, she wasn't altogether sure she was being wise.

Later, as she went to bed that night, she wondered why

she had worried. Brad had been his most charming self, doing everything he could to please her. He had teased her lightly, looked deep into her eyes and held her hand, and had seemed unaware that his strong, warm thigh had been close to hers throughout dinner. After they left the restaurant he had taken her to the top of their favourite hill to enjoy the moonlight, but again he had just held her hand and kissed her lightly.

Yet when at last she fell asleep it was to dream she was in his arms, and he was holding her tightly, in an embrace which was gentle at first but became intensely urgent. In her sleep she found herself clinging to him, murmuring his name, but she couldn't seem to make out what he said when he replied. The dream was so real it woke her up, and to her dismay she found she was alone. Apart from herself there was no one else in the bedroom.

CHAPTER TWO

WHEN Brad picked them up next morning he seemed pre-occupied, and Julie, remembering he was taking another girl out that evening, was rather silent herself. The woman whom he had been talking to in his house as she'd left last night could be another of his special friends, and she wondered bleakly how many more there might be. What real chance did she have of holding his interest in the face of such competition? She had a horrible feeling that Brad's friendship, which she tried to convince herself was all she wanted, could be removed from her at any moment now.

In the days which followed, however, she began to believe her fears to be groundless. He continued to ring her at the office. Once he even arrived there in person, after he had arranged to pick her up early. Speculation, Julie knew, was rife, and, although in her more serious moments she wished he would be more discreet, she would have been less than human if she hadn't got a little satisfaction from the envious attention this brought her. Elsa, one of the girls she worked with, even went as far as to ask teasingly when the wedding was to be.

Before Julie could tell her not to be so silly, an older girl interrupted, 'That's what I call a stupid question, Elsa. Men like Brad Hewson don't marry girls like us.'

'Well, he certainly seems fond enough of Julie!'

Margery Brown shrugged. 'All men enjoy the chase, my dear, and he'd not be the first to be caught by a pair of attractive legs and beautifully innocent blue eyes. But he'd probably run a mile if he heard wedding bells. He might not have the same objections to bed, though—not from what I hear! Has he asked you to go to bed with him yet, Julie?'

'Of course not! Julie cried indignantly, her face hot.

The other girl laughed maliciously. 'Don't worry, darling, he'll soon get round to it, you'll see.'

Julie had tried to take no notice, but it had taken some long, hard thinking before she had got rid of her suspicions that Margery Brown could be right. If Brad had wanted an affair with her, wouldn't he have done something about it before now? He had been taking her out for almost a month. Men who only wanted an affair didn't, from what she'd heard, waste that kind of time. No, Margery was wrong! Not that Julie expected wedding bells, but surely it wasn't too far-fetched, not even in these days, for a man and a girl to be just friends, with perhaps a few casual kisses thrown in? And, as Brad had only once kissed her in any other way, she didn't think this was anything to be alarmed about.

As for marriage, Julie wasn't certain that this appealed to her any more than it probably did to Brad. She liked him, but there was a big difference in their ages, as well, she suspected, in experience. Friendship was one thing, marriage another. The former, Julie decided she could cope with, but somehow she couldn't see herself married to a man like Brad Hewson. Possibly, in her wildest, most secret moments, when she allowed her romantic imagination full rein, she might, but never when she was her normal, sensible self.

While they appeared to have a lot in common and could always find plenty to talk about, Julie was quite aware of her limitations. When it came to running a big house and entertaining business colleagues, she could be lost. She had had a good education, even if she hadn't been able to find a job in the exact sphere for which she had been trained, but hadn't travelled. Nor was she in any way familiar with the sophisticated circles she believed Brad moved in. No, in the unlikely event of Brad proposing, she would have to turn him down, but at least it

would be he who would be going around looking glum—
not Julie Gray!

Unfortunately Julie's astute summing up of the situation
proved far from correct, and she was only to be protected
from the realisation of this for a few more days.

It had been a rather wonderful week. Brad and she had
been out together most evenings and he hadn't stinted the
expense. He took her to some very exclusive places to eat
and they saw some wonderful shows. She had felt quietly
happy about everything—until he gave her the earrings.
When he presented them to her she had felt startled. Her
eyes widening, she had shaken her head and began protesting that they were too expensive. Foreboding descended
like a weight on her spirits with the horrible suspicion that
the stones were real diamonds.

'I'd rather you didn't buy me presents like this, Brad,'
she had said hesitantly, not caring to use the word costly,
for fear they were not, and she would be made to feel
more naïve than she already felt. She knew little about
jewellery, certainly not enough to assess its value. The
earrings might only look expensive.

Brad merely laughed at her, but when she continued
to shake her head his expression had changed to one of
angry impatience. It was then that she gave in. She even
allowed him to fix them to her small, well-shaped ears,
shivering as his lips pressed warmly beside the coldness
of the glittering stones.

He had mistaken her reaction. 'I'm kissing you, not your
earrings,' he smiled, staring into her bemused eyes, before
adding something that kept coming back to her afterwards,
which on reflection she found strangely disturbing. 'There's
a matching necklace where these come from, Julie. You
might have it one day, as a kind of bonus, if you try to make
me happy.'

What had he meant? With his mouth insistent on her
throat, his arms sliding gently around her, she couldn't do

more than wonder fleetingly. Obviously a reckoning was to be demanded, but held to him so adoringly, she put the suspicion from her. It was later that the words came back to haunt her dreams.

If this troubled her, what he said to Joe, a few days after this, troubled Julie even more.

This morning Brad called for them and, as Julie sank into the soft leather seats, she thought how lovely it was to be able to travel to work in such comfort. Whenever she thought of going back to catching buses she felt a curious reluctance, and deliberately closed her mind to the indisputable fact that this couldn't go on for ever. Her own feelings weren't getting any easier to decipher and Brad seemed sometimes strangely on edge, for all he kept their relationship casual. In spite of his occasionally deeper caresses, the coldness of uncertainty often touched Julie's heart.

'It's getting quite cold in the mornings, now.' She turned to Brad a pink, glowing face, speaking brightly, in an effort to chase away her sudden depression.

He nodded, studying her appreciatively, for as long as it was safe in the moving car. As their eyes locked she heard Joe's agitated cough, then his advice to Brad to watch where he was going.

Brad smiled, taking his eyes from Julie to study the road. Trembling slightly, Julie didn't move, not until he spoke to Joe again.

'I'm thinking of taking a break shortly, Joe. Somehow the summer's got over and I haven't managed to get away. With all the industrial unrest we've been having it wouldn't have been easy, but I think things are more settled just now. I thought I'd better mention it, so you can make other arrangements for getting to work.'

'I'm glad to hear you're considering a holiday at last,' Joe replied formally. 'And you don't have to worry about me. I'm buying a new car.'

Between Brad's news and Joe's, Julie felt stunned. Brad

was going away almost immediately and Joe was buying a new car! She didn't know whom to turn to first. Feeling on safer ground, she turned to her stepfather. 'How can you be buying a new car, Joe? You can't afford it! I mean —that is . . .' Suddenly embarrassed, she broke off, looking quickly at Brad. She shouldn't have spoken to Joe like this in front of Brad. 'I—are you going anywhere special, Brad?' she faltered.

'It depends,' he replied enigmatically, without taking his eyes from the road.

Joe said quickly, as though he sensed the slight strain in the atmosphere, 'You haven't been to London for a while?'

'I send Smith.' Brad jammed on the brakes to avoid a suicidal pedestrian. 'I'll be there more in future, I hope. I'm thinking of closing the house down for the winter.'

When Julie left the car at the works she felt so chilled she scarcely knew what she was doing. It wasn't until after he had gone that she realised Brad hadn't said anything about picking her up that evening. This, along with the news he had so casually imparted, could mean only one thing. It spelled the end of their relationship, as such, in large capital letters! For one earth-shattering moment, Julie felt so terrible she thought she was going to be sick.

All day she fretted, hope fighting the hopelessness within her until she feared she would be torn in two. Brad didn't ring and she went home on the bus, wondering if she looked as dreadful as she felt. She tried to cheer up, but it wasn't easy.

Joe, for once, was home before her. She was surprised to find him having tea with Edith. They were both in the kitchen drinking out of the pretty pottery mugs Julie had bought with her first salary. Immediately she offered to make sandwiches and suggested they take the whole lot into the lounge.

They refused, or rather Joe did. Edith stood where she was, smiling happily, while Joe explained that he had asked Edith to marry him, and she had accepted.

Julie was delighted. It could be the best thing for Joe as he must have been lonely since her mother died. Pushing her own unhappiness to one side, she congratulated them warmly. She liked Edith, who taught in the village school, and was a greatly respected member of the community. Edith was about the same age as Joe, so they would be able to enjoy their retirement together. And it would leave her free. Free for what? she wondered dismally.

'Listen, chick,' said Joe, after they had had a drink and the excitement had died down. 'We were thinking of having a celebration, I actually have the table booked. How about asking Brad to join us?'

'Oh, I don't know, Joe. Brad might be busy. Besides, this is a family occasion.' She didn't say he hadn't brought her home.

Joe ignored what she had said about family. 'Why not give him the chance?' he smiled teasingly.

Because she couldn't find another excuse, without mentioning things she wasn't yet ready to talk about, Julie went slowly to the telephone. Suddenly she was glad Joe had made her. There might be nothing to worry about. Brad might not have meant all he had said that morning and tonight he might simply have been held up. He worked long hours, and there were board meetings and union meetings which often went on for hours—days and weeks, sometimes.

It wasn't sensible, she cautioned herself sternly, to grasp the telephone as though her life depended on it. Deliberately she forced her tense fingers to slacken.

Brad's manservant answered. 'Could I speak to Mr Hewson?' she asked breathlessly. 'Julie Gray speaking.'

'I'm sorry, Miss Gray. Mr Hewson has just left.'

'I—I see. Do you know, Mr Foster, if he intended coming here?'

Foster cleared his throat, a habit he had, she had discovered, when he wasn't quite sure what to say. 'A—

someone called, Miss Gray, and I believe he'll be out all evening. They left about an hour ago.'

'Thank you ...'

For a few minutes Julie stayed where she was, feeling sick again but trying to impress on herself the need to act calmly. This sort of thing happened to girls every day, and it wasn't as if she had been totally unprepared for it. A man like Brad Hewson would naturally soon tire of a girl like herself, although she liked to think their friendship had been a good one.

If it was a rather awkward threesome, neither Joe nor Edith appeared to notice. Joe had his new car and a new fiancée and was bubbling over with high spirits. Joe's new car might have worried Julie more if she hadn't been so numb with unhappiness over Brad. Where Joe had got the money from puzzled her. He might have borrowed, but she couldn't think of anyone in a position to loan him over five thousand pounds. His bank manager might, but she doubted it, not on Joe's previous performance. Repaying the interest alone would be more than he could manage. His holidays, his taste in clothes had always been extravagant, but she could never remember him going as far as this before.

Edith must be helping out, that was all Julie could think of. It seemed logical, as she and Joe were getting married, but somehow Julie didn't care for the idea. Ah well, Joe was Edith's responsibility now. If she decided Joe spent too freely, then it was up to her to put a stop to it.

If Brad had been with them Julie would have enjoyed the evening, with her feeling of pending release from Joe's rather irresponsible ways. But Brad wasn't there and the hours went slowly, without excitement.

It wasn't until the next evening, after a day of almost unendurable sly digs at the office, that he got in touch. She knew he was still at the works, as Joe had mentioned it, but she had grown resigned and was bracing herself to sit out the barrage of malicious teasing which would certainly descend on her head, once it became known definitely that Brad had dropped her.

When the telephone rang she stared at it for several seconds before finding the courage to answer it. She told herself it wouldn't be Brad, that she hoped it wasn't, while aware of praying almost feverishly that it was. Contemptuously she made herself pause and think. What use was a man who ignored a girl and then picked her up, just when he felt like it?

At last, unable to resist temptation any longer, she lifted the receiver with trembling hands. Swallowing an obstruction in her throat, she gave her name.

It was Brad. 'I was just about to give up,' he said, 'I thought you must be out.'

Julie's voice shook, nearly as badly as her hands. Taking a deep breath, she managed to insert a note of cool surprise. 'Brad!' she exclaimed. 'Why, hello.'

'No more enthusiasm than that?' he teased softly.

Resentment suddenly stiffened her. 'I can't very well throw my arms around a telephone, even if I wanted to!' she retorted sarcastically.

'You don't sound too sure.'

'Perhaps I'm not.' There was a peculiar warmth spreading inside her, thawing the chill of the past few days, but resentment was still uppermost.

'Hum,' he laughed. 'That wasn't what I wanted to hear.'

Julie strove to stay calm. 'Did you want anything, specially, Brad, or were you just ringing to say goodbye again? If so I won't keep you, as you're probably in a hurry to get off on your holiday?'

'I didn't say I was leaving immediately.' He sounded very reasonable. He made it seem as though she was the one who was not.

Could he be right? Distractedly Julie hesitated. It was only her pride which had been hurt, it wasn't as if she loved him. Or was it? Taking another deep breath, which she hoped would sweep such thoughts right out of her mind, she muttered, 'Well, this week, next week—what's the difference?'

'You'd be. surprised!' Then the laughter left his voice and he was suddenly serious. 'Listen, Julie Gray, I've booked a table at your favourite restaurant for dinner. Can you be ready in, say, fifteen minutes?'

'Just like that?' she gasped.

'Oh, come on, Julie. I haven't time for sulks. I'm in a hurry to see you again.'

'I'm not sulking!' She wanted to make that quite clear. If what he said last made her pulse race, it could only be with anger.

'Yes or no?' he asked, so decisively that she couldn't pretend not to know what he was talking about.

At the very moment it shouldn't, her nerve failed her. 'Yes,' she heard herself muttering despairingly, then hoped to cancel her regrettable weakness by putting the phone down immediately.

Brad arrived, as he had stated he would, exactly fifteen minutes later. Julie, feeling tense to the point of exhaustion from the turmoil inside her, was ready, but only just. Trying to be rational about their relationship wasn't a simple process, but she had reached a decision. Tonight she would tell him she wasn't going out with him again. It would be wiser to make the break before she grew any fonder of him. A girl didn't have to suffer from a broken heart, if she was sensible.

Brad was waiting in the sitting-room, talking with Joe. In the doorway she paused, a slender, attractive girl in a blue dress, her silky hair falling sleek and shining over her shoulders, a faint smile touching the candid sweetness of her mouth. If she looked young, it was because she was, but her elegance was inbred. She would always have it, this and her fine bone structure, which drew so much flattering attention, especially from men.

Brad smiled at her lazily, as Joe quickly excused himself to go and meet Edith. 'Hello, Julie.' His smile disappeared as she stepped aside to let Joe pass. Coming towards her, he held her eyes intently, until her heart began beating rapidly. He took both her hands in his and kissed them, before putting a firm arm around her shoulders to draw her close.

'Missed me?'

'Yes, Brad.' Feeling his lips against her hair, that was all she could think of, how much she had missed him. Then, remembering hastily she hadn't been going to let him know, she tacked on quickly, 'Sometimes.'

Putting his knuckles under her chin, he smiled again as he considered her cross little face. 'You meant to be annoyed with me but you forgot? Will it do if I apologise? I want you to be happy.'

'You don't have to apologise, Brad,' she said bravely, only too well aware he had little to apologise for. They had just been friendly. Apart from once or twice he had scarcely even held her hand. It was merely the inadvertent publicity, because he was head of the firm, which would hurt when they split up. 'You don't have to tell me or anyone, I suppose, what you're doing.'

'I've been busy.' He spoke so curtly she was startled. His arm tightened around her shoulders and, looking up at him, she was drawn into a kind of breathless silence.

'You say you missed me?' he persisted, his voice thickening. And when she nodded mutely, he dropped a quick kiss on her uncertain mouth. 'I've missed you so much, Julie, these last two days, I don't want to think about it.'

'Brad ...?' His arm was warm around her but did nothing to stop her trembling.

'Let's go.' His grey eyes probed deeply before he turned her abruptly around. 'There's something we have to talk about, but if we stay here any longer I'm going to forget all about the chat.'

Julie wasn't sure if she enjoyed the meal or not. Brad was in a strange mood, often withdrawn. Sometimes when he looked at her she could make nothing of his arrogant, indifferent expression. He made no attempt to explain what he had been doing over the last two days which made her wonder if he had really been as busy as he had made out.

'You haven't been very hungry?' He frowned, when she refused the sweet trolley and cheese and pushed her coffee cup away.

'No,' she agreed reluctantly, 'I wasn't as hungry as I thought I was.' She lifted her eyes to his, wide blue eyes which held a trace of apology. Audibly she sighed as bewilderment chased pensive shadows over her beautiful face, as though she had unsolved problems which were worrying her desperately

'Would you care to dance?' Brad asked quietly, without removing his eyes from hers. He didn't seem to have looked anywhere else during dinner, and this attention, though not she suspected always kind, had aroused a dangerous kind of intimacy. It made Julie conscious of the fluid, aching desire she felt for him. As she nodded mutely and stood up, she was hazily aware she could be putty in his hands, if she wasn't careful.

She hadn't given it much thought, but she and Brad had danced a lot lately. It was just one of the things they enjoyed doing together, but dancing seemed to have become something rather special. A certain magic was to be found in his arms, although she tried not to think of it. Dreamily she decided it lay in the clasp of their hands, the touch of hips and thighs, the closeness of their bodies as they swayed to the music. Whatever the cause, there was a strange, almost tangible excitement when they were together like this, that drew them closer and closer.

Brad was no mean performer on the dance floor, no matter what the orchestra was playing. It made Julie wonder, with some misgivings, how many other girls had shared the delight she was experiencing now. He held her tonight as if they had been parted for much longer than a few days, his hands warm on her waist and shoulders, his cheek against hers. When it came to the third dance, with the lights lowered on the crowded floor and his arms tightened, Julie's heavy lashes fell and she trembled. Urgently she tried to resist the flood of longing he unleashed in her.

Because he was tall and well made, she liked the feel of his hard muscles against the softness of her own body. He was rugged, but he moved with the supple smoothness of a jungle animal, and always she followed his lead. Yet tonight he stumbled twice and once he swore softly under his breath.

Eventually he said, 'It's after midnight, Julie, and there's something I want to ask you. Shall we go?'

What kind of question did a man find so urgent at this time of night? Only one, Julie decided, scarcely daring to even let it cross her mind. Nor did she dare think what kind of answer she would give him, if she was right. She wasn't sure if she loved him enough to marry him. Her heart might whisper she did, but she wasn't really sure what love was. She would have to be very sure.

Brad stopped the car on a secluded spot, well off the road, where they would be free from interruptions. Turning to her, he flicked her seat back before drawing her into his arms. 'Come here,' he said softly.

The desire to know what it was he wanted to talk to her about faded before the more urgent one inside her to cling to him. As his arms went around her they were sure and strong. A decisiveness flowed from him which was very reassuring to her less confident nature. As she gazed up at him, his face, lean and tough-looking, came nearer and she made no attempt to avoid his seeking mouth. She gave a soft murmur, a mixture of fear and delight, then heard him utter something before he began kissing her. His mouth hardened as he bruised her soft lips in a cruel kiss that seemed to go on and on.

Julie, feeling swept by the leaping flames of a fire, sought instinctively to respond but found it impossible. His mouth crushed her head back until she thought her slender neck might snap and he held her so tightly she couldn't move. Then, as his passion increased, he released her slightly, so his hands might have access to the rounded curves of her body. When he released her shaking mouth she was so breathlessly disturbed she couldn't speak.

'Show me how much you've missed me?' Through the pale light his face was enigmatically watchful as he looked straight in her eyes. 'Now it's your turn,' he challenged.

'How ...?' But even as she asked, some strange being inside her was taking over, making her reach up to press quivering lips compulsively against his. It seemed, somehow, the most natural thing in the world to be doing, to be kissing him like this, to be pleasing him while at the same time pleasing herself. As her heart warmed to him, Julie was dazzled by the force of her own feelings.

She knew she hadn't the expertise to keep it up, but Brad's low laughter was triumphant as he gradually took over, his hands and mouth instructing slowly but with a tantalising precision. That she had obviously a lot to learn seemed only to fill him with satisfaction. His first urgency passed—or was being held well under control, but he was arousing them both, in a different way. Suddenly, vaguely warned that this new approach could hold more danger than his former ruthlessness, Julie stiffened on a broken murmur of protest and pulled away from him.

'Julie ...' he allowed her to go just so far. His arms still enfolded her as he groaned against her throbbing breast. 'I want you so much, my dear. I want you to come and live with me, be my mistress, if you like. This is what I wanted to ask you.'

'You ... Your—what?' Julie was so startled she couldn't get the word out. Sickly she recoiled, while praying shakenly that she had misunderstood.

When Brad lifted his dark head, she saw his mouth quirk wryly on her stunned face, 'I realise there are more tactful ways of putting it, but I usually believe in being frank. Pretty words, delightful phrases shouldn't always be used to disguise the truth, and I think you would prefer me to be honest with you. I've wanted you since the first time we met.' His voice thickened as he looked down at her. 'I can't remember ever wanting a woman so much.'

A chill fear spreading through her, Julie licked her dry lips with her tongue. If she hadn't done so she couldn't have spoken. 'You're asking me to live with you, Brad, at Haydon Hill?'

He smiled at this, as if she was being incredibly foolish but he forgave her because she was young and very lovely. 'Not at Haydon Hill, sweetheart. Not even at my flat in London. I'll find you a flat in London, but one of your own. I'll look after you, naturally, but it will be easier if we don't live together.'

'Easier to get rid of me when you tire of our association, you mean?' The shock of hurt really painful now, Julie dragged herself from his arms. 'I'm sorry, Brad,' she said bleakly. 'I just couldn't ...'

'What's that supposed to mean?' He didn't attempt to take hold of her again. From his face, Julie guessed he was trying carefully not to upset her. It held all the calculating vigour of a man intent on getting his own way, but was too much of a diplomat to use force. 'Do you mean,' he asked, 'that you would if you felt you had only yourself to please, but that you're frightened of Joe, and what people might say?'

She looked at him, at the expressive mouth, the cautious glint in his dark grey eyes, the smoulder of desire replacing this as his glance flicked over her, a desire he made little attempt to hide. Looking at him, she wondered what it would be like to live with him, but found it impossible to visualise. Only the sudden race of her pulse gave her a clue.

'If I wanted to do this, Brad, I wouldn't be frightened of what people would say. Joe—well, yes, I suppose he would count, but that wasn't what I meant.'

'What, then?'

While she bitterly considered his deliberate patience, he went on, 'You didn't think I'd ask you to live with me here, did you? I'm not such a thoughtless fool as that. You'll live in London, and I'll be there at least two nights a week.'

'Two nights a week!'

He sighed, touching her hair gently, as though he liked the feel of it. 'We could see how we got on. I think I mentioned, the other morning, that I'm thinking of closing Haydon Hill up for the winter, so you'd probably see quite a lot of me. To begin with, anyway,' his voice deepened to a husky growl as his eyes examined her moon-tinted features, 'I can't see myself ever getting tired of you, though.'

'What,' she gasped, feeling wildly provoked by such bland condescension, 'would I be supposed to do all day, to fill my time in?'

'You could always get a job, if you feel bored, but I can almost guarantee you won't, not for a long time. I mean to be a very demanding lover.'

All at once, Julie found herself shaking. It was like a bad dream. She had received a proposal, all right, but it was far from what she had expected! A hysterical giggle rose in her throat, she had to press her lips together to suppress it, and she felt herself grow colder. From Brad's point of view, she supposed, it would be an ideal set-up, and one he was familiar with. How many girls, over the years, had he lived with? He intended being generous with both his time and money and considered she had nothing to complain of. He seemed so sure of the outcome, she could see it in the amused tolerance of his expression. He believed she wouldn't find it possible to refuse him.

Her thoughts raced, with such speed she couldn't seem to stop them, until one, much worse than the rest, brought them to a sudden halt. Had this been the reason for Brad's recent neglect? Had he deliberately tried to make her so distraught she would agree to anything?

Lifting her silky head, she met his eyes despairingly. 'Is this what you've been planning, over the past few days, Brad?'

His mouth thinned, as some of her reluctance got through to him at last. 'No. I said I was busy and it was the truth, but it did occur to me that it was a breathing space we both needed, if just to take stock.'

'And you decided you wanted me to live with you?'

'Yes.' His hand on her chin lifted it towards him. His head came down, she gave a little moan which she couldn't suppress as his lips took hers. In Julie ecstasy was born at his touch and she knew it would take very little to persuade her to his will. The melting, rapturous emotion dissolved all her efforts to resist him. His arms became a delightful prison and she delighted in the bruising ardour of his mouth. In a very few moments she was responding to the warmth of his passion and unable to hide it.

'Does that answer your question?' He kept her close, his hand caressing the smooth skin of her arm as it lay against his shoulder, before sliding proprietorially to the curve of her breast. It was the first time he had done this, and the sensation he aroused wasn't immediately bearable. A small, involuntary gasp escaped her, as she flinched. He laughed, the low laughter of a man certain of victory. 'Well?' he asked.

Praying he would never know what it cost her, Julie shook her silken head. 'I'm sorry, Brad. I thought you'd realised I'm not that kind of girl.'

'I know you aren't, sweetheart.' His lean mouth twisted mockingly. 'None of you ever are, but having got that bit out of the way how about a straight answer?'

His arrogance made her furious. 'You expected me to jump at the chance, of course?'

'Yes, since you ask.'

This shocked her so much she struggled violently against his hold on her. 'I'm sorry I have to refuse.' Her face was white.

'Julie!' He was suddenly grim, his chiselled features harsh; she had a ringside glimpse of a man well used to settling disputes of a greater magnitude than he considered this to be. He leant nearer, so she was disturbed by the clean, masculine scent of him, half lost as his eyes looked straight in hers. 'Julie, I want you to think about this very carefully. I'll give you time.'

'No, thank you, Brad,' her anger was spent and she felt on the verge of tears, 'I don't need any time. Even if I live to be a hundred, my answer to this kind of proposal will always be the same.'

'God!' His brows lifted with cynical amusement. 'You weren't expecting a proposal of marriage, were you?'

That hurt—and humiliated—yet she found herself being foolishly honest. 'I thought that might be what you—you had in mind. But I was mistaken.'

'You can say that again,' he said coldly. 'I don't care for being tied.'

Julie smiled, a little sadly, looking away from the taunting fascination of his eyes to stare blindly out at the encroaching darkness of the night. Her fingers clenched despondently. 'If you'd asked me to marry you, it doesn't follow I'd have jumped at that either.'

'No. Maybe either way you're too frigid to want to get that near a man.'

They both knew that wasn't true. In his arms, Julie had felt and betrayed a profound excitement. Brad knew about it, all right; she could sense it was that, as much as anything, that was making him wholly determined to have her. His fingers bit into her arm and a violence he was controlling made her shiver, but she refused to give in.

'Julie,' he made another attempt to win her over, his voice kinder, 'why not take my advice before definitely rejecting my offer? I'm not the marrying kind, but that doesn't mean I don't know how to treat a woman. I'm willing to swear you'll want for nothing, and you won't have any complaints about me as a lover. You'll be more than content—I guarantee.'

Such expertise could only be acquired by experience, but who was she to reproach him? Any criticism she might level would only be brushed carelessly aside. Bitterly she retorted, 'Some women require more than that. A husband and family must surely come first.'

'You could easily find a husband.'

'After you'd finished with me, I suppose?'

His eyes narrowed. 'There are plenty of men who would be very pleased to marry you.'

Choking through tears, she cried, her eyes blazing, 'You think I'd go to a husband second-hand?'

'Oh, save us!' He ran terse fingers through his thick, dark hair. 'Do you really think anyone bothers about that sort of thing today?'

Her voice wobbled, but she managed to say, 'You wouldn't care?'

'I'm not here to be catechised, Julie Gray, as to my views on virginity.'

Suddenly she guessed he would care, one day. But it wouldn't be her finger that would receive his ring, while the Wedding March played softly.

'I don't care what you think, or say,' she said, almost defiantly, 'I have certain standards which I believe in, and when I marry it will be for love.'

'Love,' he laughed harshly, 'is for poets and dreamers, Julie Gray. It has nothing to do with practicalities.'

'Then I can't have finished with dreams yet.' Pain stirred in her, a sick sense of disappointment. Suddenly she knew she must get away from him, to find somewhere quiet to lick her wounds. 'Please take me home, Brad,' she pleaded.

Obligingly he started the engine, his movements savage, unusually unco-ordinated. Thinly he said, 'I'll be here for a few more days. If you should happen to change your mind you know where to find me.' Grimly he turned his head to look straight at her. 'It might pay to remember,

Julie, that we do have something going between us. If I choose to exert pressure you wouldn't stand a chance.'

'I have my pride, Brad,' she rejected him fiercely, agony curling within her as she wondered if she was doing the right thing.

'Pride won't keep you warm at nights,' he flung back cryptically, his glance full of cold mockery as he released the brake and they slid out on to the road.

CHAPTER THREE

JOE'S car wasn't in the garage and the house was silent as Julie let herself in and ran upstairs. She was used now to having Brad unlock the door for her when Joe was out, used to having him wait until she put on the light, before he went. Young as Julie was, she found the feeling of being cherished hard to do without, once she had grown accustomed to it.

In her bedroom she took off her dress, concentrating on that, with the undue care of one in shock, rather than think of Brad and what had just taken place between them. As she slid into bed she despaired that she couldn't keep his image at bay any longer. He haunted her with a persistence she found impossible to reject completely.

He had asked her to live with him, and while she considered it an insult she had seen that he had imagined he was paying her a great compliment. Which, in a way, was difficult to understand as he hadn't seemed surprised at her obvious disgust. Of course, as he apparently viewed her reaction as the initial feminine one to such a suggestion, that would account for his lack of astonishment. Afterwards, she sensed, he had been angrier than he let it appear, and for all he said he would wait for her to change her mind she fancied he wouldn't be willing to wait indefinitely. Many other girls would be only too eager to give him what he so arrogantly demanded, without him having to beg.

Julie sighed and tossed in her bed, a sob in her throat, her slim body burning as her half awakened emotions continued to taunt her. When Brad kissed her all her senses came alive and she knew it would be very easy to allow him to make love to her. He aroused her curiosity about the deeper relationships shared by men and women, that which lay beyond a few casual kisses. Oh, yes, it would be very easy to give in to Brad Hewson, but she couldn't go against every principle she had been brought up to believe in.

But wouldn't you settle for anything, a small voice whispered, rather than face an empty future without him? No, she replied, because she wasn't sure that she loved him, and this could have been the only possible excuse. The heavy, painful ache in her heart couldn't be love; regret, perhaps, and the almost bereft feeling of knowing he despised her, but never love. Love surely only throve when fed on warmth and respect and, looking back, Julie decided Brad had shown her little of either. Sudden tears overwhelming her, she clutched her pillow tightly as she began to sob. She couldn't remember ever being so unhappy, not since her mother died.

Twice, in the distance, during the days that followed, she caught sight of Brad, that was all, but she found even a fleeting glimpse of his dark, handsome head disturbing. There was absolutely no contact between them and Julie, finding herself hungering desperately for some sign of recognition, was sometimes sorely tempted to pick up the telephone and present him with an unconditional surrender. Yet, surprisingly, she struggled with her deep inclinations and won. If she did as he asked she was sure she would never be able to live happily with her conscience, and a lack of such happiness would surely destroy any possibility of them remaining long together.

In the typing pool, one of the girls announced her engagement, and another got herself into the kind of trouble which, unfortunate or otherwise, helped strengthen Julie's wavering resolutions. For a short while the limelight was centred on others, the breathing space bridging the gap that yawned between her last meeting with Brad and his imperious summons to his office. When he rang for her to go she was reluctant.

She wanted to protest, refuse, plead illness, anything

which might excuse her from going, but realising it would only draw unwelcome attention, she obeyed.

On her way to Brad's office her legs felt so weak she found it difficult to walk the few yards from the lift to his door. What could he want to see her about? He had told her to get in touch, if she changed her mind, but her silence must have demonstrated her refusal to do this. By now he must have realised it was a hopeless subject to pursue. Julie's wide, smooth brow creased as her thoughts floundered. Could it be about Joe? She hadn't mentioned that Joe was thinking of getting married, when Brad had last taken her out. She had meant to tell him, before leaving him that night, but as things had turned out she had forgotten. A long strand of shining hair escaped the neat coil which she wore for work, and with impatient fingers she brushed it back. No, it was unlikely to be Joe. Joe's personal life could be of no concern to Brad.

Knocking feebly, she entered the outer office. Inside, his secretary, along with her two assistants, were just finishing for the day. They already had their coats on and the assistants stared at Julie with undisguised interest. His secretary smiled as she picked up her handbag, her free hand indicating Brad's door, telling Julie to go in.

'Mr Hewson is expecting you.'

'Thank you ...'

Julie opened Brad's door and went through it, without being fully conscious of walking over the few yards of carpet. He was sitting at his desk, his head bowed as he twiddled abstractedly with a pen he held in both hands, but he rose politely, coming towards her, ushering her in then closing the door again.

'Hello, Julie. How are you?'

She had to let out the deep breath she had been holding so could manage no more than a faint smile. The smile wasn't genuine, but she hoped he wouldn't guess. It was merely to cover up.

He halted abruptly, staring down at her as though he

must see her closely. Her eyes drawn to him against her will, she saw he looked haggard. He seemed older, and curiously strained. Obviously he was in need of the holiday he had so far done without.

Because the silence became uncomfortable, Julie sought for something to say. 'I'm—I'm quite well, Brad.'

'Are you?'

She thought he was about to add that it was more than he was, but his jaw hardened, as if he guessed what she was thinking and wanted to deny it.

'I've been expecting you.' His voice was harsh, his eyes beginning to glitter. He didn't ask her to sit down. As her bewildered glance pointedly found the nearest chair he took no notice, and she couldn't mention the regrettable state of her legs.

Julie had to clear her throat twice, it felt so uncomfortable. 'I don't think that's quite fair. You told me to get in touch if I had something to tell you.'

'And you have nothing?'

How angry he looked! He almost managed to terrify her, but not enough to make her whisper what she suddenly suspected he desperately wanted to hear. Work in the offices had mostly stopped for the day. The silence around them alarmed Julie as it made her realise how alone Brad and she were up here. Twice she tried to speak and failed. In the end she just shook her head.

'I see.'

Still staring at her intently, his eyes went over her slim, tense figure before resting on her pale face. Then, to her surprise, he stalked grimly to the window where he stood for a moment gazing out, before closing it. Once he had told her he liked having a window open as he didn't care over much for central heating. Naturally he wouldn't want to leave it open all night, but she had an uneasy feeling he was just using this as an excuse. He had wanted a few seconds to think.

As she saw him silhouetted against the darkness, her

breath caught as she found herself studying his height and breadth of shoulder. Some time during the afternoon, he had discarded his jacket and loosened his tie. As he turned back to her she could detect his curling body hair through the thinness of his silk shirt, see the dark shadow of it at his throat. He rminded her of a virile, dangerous animal, prowling on silent feet in search of its prey.

Nor was she far wrong. As he came towards her again, the eyes boring into hers held a positive glitter, which spoke, as before, of anger only barely held in check. With clear insight Julie realised Brad's pride was suffering, and he considered her responsible. He had asked her to come and see him, expecting her to fall weeping in his arms. The superb confidence which had secured for him almost all he had wanted from life until now had suffered a severe blow, one which he was finding almost impossible to accept.

It was this last impression that made Julie really anxious. She wished suddenly that she could put her arms around him and soothe him. Rashly, for all her racing pulse, she might have done if instinct hadn't warned this could be putting a match to a keg of dynamite.

Having no experience of such a situation to draw on, she could only murmur helplessly, 'You didn't have to send for me, Mr Hewson.'

In that moment she didn't find it difficult to be formal. Brad was almost a stranger in his fury, but her softly spoken words didn't have the desired effect. The use of his surname only appeared to incense him further.

Harshly he countered, while tearing open another button of his shirt, as if to breathe better, 'I've been watching you since our last little get-together, Julie. In asking to see you today, I believed I was doing you a favour. A blind man could see how you were suffering, and only a fool would let it continue any longer. I took into account your pride, which I'm convinced is the only thing that stopped you coming to me, but you must allow me a little pride, too, my dear. You can't expect me to go down on my hands and knees. If I have to use further persuasion to make you see sense, it won't be that way.'

Julie, feeling sick that her unhappiness had been so obvious, felt her own temper rising and tried to restrain it. It wouldn't do to risk making the situation more dangerous than it already was. Nevertheless, her rebellious tongue wasn't to be controlled that easily, and her dazzling blue eyes, wide with defiance, resisted his black glance. 'You must be mad if you think I'd fall for your cheap proposition. I've been hating you, not fretting for you!'

'You're lying!' His usually well modulated voice was so curt it grated. 'I know how you respond to me, and I should be able to judge. I know about women.'

'I realise,' Julie cried shrilly, hurt whipping up her anger to a frenzy, 'you've had plenty of practice—but not with me!'

Now he was gripping her shoulders. From the look in his eyes she feared he was going to slap her. 'I refuse to be made a fool of, Julie. I might have the most experience, but it could be debatable. You're a little tease.'

That did it. She felt her temper explode, as she could never remember it doing before. Her hands flew up as she tried to hit him, claw at his face, but Brad only swore and grasped her wrists. She might have been waving paper banners, so ineffective was she.

Humiliated beyond everything, she shouted hoarsely, her small face scarlet, 'I'm not the one who's obsessed by sex, it's you! All along I think you've schemed to get your own way. You've positively showered me with gifts and outings, between dropping me and picking me up!' Her voice croaked as she drew a deep, sobbing breath, but she couldn't stop. 'You blew hot and cold deliberately, just to get me to agree to anything!' She paused on a furious little sniffle. 'You might have done, you almost did, but thank God I came to my senses in time. You're despicable and—and I want nothing more to do with you. Anyway, you couldn't make me want you now, if you tried!'

An ominous silence was momentary. Anger leapt to his eyes, scorching her. Never had she seen him so furious or suspected the primitive emotions that lay beneath his polished, sophisticated demeanour. She wanted to go on defying him, but quelled by his white hot anger, she was rendered to silence.

'You seem very sure of your ability to control your emotions,' he snarled contemptuously, while poised with a frightening rigidity of body.

Her mouth dry, Julie knew instantly she had gone too far. Another man might have allowed her to get away with such insults, but not Brad Hewson. His sensitivity to the situation was shown in his tight-lipped anger and hearing his harshly indrawn breath she panicked. Fear gave her the immediate strength to take him by surprise, to jerk away from him, but only for a second. With the reflex of a man in perfect physical condition he hauled her back. Ruthlessly his arms caught her and though she struggled desperately she couldn't escape again.

On closer contact with him than she had ever been before, Julie was suddenly very conscious of his paralysing effect.

'Brad,' she cried weakly, 'don't do anything you're going to regret.'

'Shut up!' Malignantly his eyes glittered down on her, full of black arrogance.

As he crushed her to him a cold dizziness swept over her, blotting out his satanic features as he forced her chin up towards him. A flare of light beat on her face, dazzling her as his hard mouth descended savagely upon the shaken softness of her own. There was no mercy in the lips which plundered Julie's so ruthlessly, only a harsh determination she found impossible to fight.

She wanted to fight him—she tried to wildly, but he was relentless and she could do nothing against his considerable strength. He kissed her mouth, her eyes, her hot cheeks until fire began pouring through her bloodstream, until her defiance dwindled and convulsively her arms fastened around his neck.

She heard him mutter thickly, on a low note of harsh triumph, something about winning, but not even the humiliation of this seemed able to bolster her fading resistance. Everywhere his hands touched, nerve ends quivered before returning a shattering response.

On and on he went, until she was clinging to him helplessly. Then, when he felt her pressing urgently against him, Brad lifted her in his arms, carrying her across the room to where the modern units were pushed together to form a low settee.

'I sleep here,' he growled, lowering her on to it, 'when I'm too busy to go home, but this is the first time I've used it for this purpose.'

'Brad, don't ...' Hazily aware of anger still burning harshly in him, she went white as she became conscious that her protests were futile, that for once he was driven by an emotion stronger than himself.

'Save your breath,' he taunted shortly.

Lowering her to the soft cushions, he came down beside her, and Julie could feel her heart beating wildly in her breast, like a drum. All her pulses were racing, she felt on fire, and while she knew she must go on fighting, all desire to do so was leaving her. Again he began kissing her, hot, savage kisses drained the last of her strength.

Moaning, she surrendered, returning kiss for kiss, her lips parting sensuously, her hands groping almost as urgently as his. Brad undid her blouse, his fingers dealing dextrously with buttons. Removing it, he ripped open his own shirt and threw it off, while all the while Julie watched like a girl in a trance.

Darkness descended once more as his head again shut out the light, but it was a darkness soon to be shattered by a thousand stars as his hands began exploring the tender contours of her body. His arms slid smoothly around her, easing her gently so he might undo the light fastening on her brief bra. After this was accomplished he bent and kissed her bare breasts until she thought she would faint from the heat of the wild sensation which whipped through her.

The world as she knew it exploded in thousands of glittering pieces, as the warm, sweet quiver of desire flooded her whole being. All Brad's movements, now, were slower, more deliberate, and she felt herself beginning to float through a thick mist where only the hardness of his mouth and the pressure of his arms had any reality.

It wasn't until she felt his strong limbs entangling with hers, that the cloud in her mind broke to allow her a fleeting glimpse of immediate danger.

'No, Brad!' In spite of an answering passion tearing her apart, she made a desperate attempt to evade him.

'Be still!' His voice was so slurred she could scarcely understand him. 'Do you want me to hurt you?'

'No ...' Yet something forced her to fight the desire to obey. As he bent his lips to her throat, she turned her swimming head frantically. On the table by their side was a small marble reading lamp. She grabbed it wildly, crashing it down on Brad just as he raised his head.

To her incredulous surprise it caught him on the side of his brow with a resounding thud. Afterwards, when she dared think about it, she thought it had been like a film shown in slow motion. His eyes widened in utter astonishment, then slowly closed, as with a protesting moan he slid gently sideways to the floor.

Stunned horror kept Julie momentarily frozen to the spot. Staring at Brad, she wondered wildly what she had done. Had she killed him?

'Oh, no!' she sobbed aloud. Suddenly coming to life, she scrambled from the settee to kneel beside him. Nearer she bent, her eyes glazed with terrified anguish as the blood poured down his cheek from a gaping wound on his forehead. 'Oh, no!' she cried again, her face cold with shock, so that the tears streaming down it felt hot by comparison.

Scarcely conscious of what she was doing, she touched his head with the tips of tentative fingers, brushing back a strand of thick dark hair.

'Brad darling,' she moaned, with sobs thickening, 'will you ever forgive me . . .'

It was strange and wholly alarming to see him lying so still, but the faintness of his breathing frightened her most. Automatically she reached for a paper tissue from the box of white ones that lay on the table where the lamp had been, and began dabbing around the cut gently, in an effort to stem the flow of blood. To her relief, although she didn't altogether succeed, she saw it wasn't as bad as it had at first seemed, but he would certainly have a dreadful headache in the morning.

One thing she was convinced of—she must get proper help for Brad as soon as possible. Blindly, without once taking her eyes from him, she groped her way into her bra and blouse, and was just about to get to her feet when she suddenly realised he was without his shirt.

Something told her it wouldn't do for him to be discovered up here without it. She would have to say he had fallen, but few would believe this if he were found without his shirt, naked from the waist up.

With a despairing glance she reached for it, trying carefully to ease it around his powerful shoulders. 'Oh, God,' she muttered weakly, when she was forced to take a closer hold of him to achieve this, and feeling began coursing through her again. Convinced she was going crazy, she completed the task as quickly as possible, but, after managing to fasten the buttons down the front, she had to steel herself to tuck it in. As she pushed it into the front of his trousers, her breath caught and she quickly withdrew, knowing, no matter what people might think, she could never do that for him.

Distractedly, as she drew slowly away from him, she decided he looked quite normal. People would simply conclude that his shirt had left his pants as he had fallen.

Casting one last distressed glance at him, she dived through the doorway. Outside, the corridor was empty and the lift quickly conveyed her to her own floor. Amazingly her head felt clear, she was able to work out a plan so easily she felt ashamed. That she seemed to have left the most vital part of herself in Brad's office should surely have affected her ability to think at all.

She mustn't go personally to the night-watchman. No one must suspect she had been with Brad—for Brad's sake, because of the talk it would cause. It was imperative though that she secure help for him quickly, but she must ring from the kiosk on the corner.

All the night-watchmen on this section were very good. They would know immediately what to do, even if they believed her call to be a hoax they would check. It was well known that they checked everything.

Fortunately there was no one around to notice her as she left the factory. Feeling like a traitor, for all she tried to tell herself it was Brad who had attacked her, Julie tightened the belt of her coat and ran.

The first kiosk she came to was empty; she wrenched open the door, a prayer of thankfulness on her lips. With trembling fingers she dialled the nightwatchman's office, and when he answered almost immediately she blurted out that Mr Hewson had fallen on the top floor and needed help.

'What sort of help, miss?' the man asked cautiously.

Her voice shook, for all she had thought to have it under control. 'If I knew,' she cried indiscreetly, 'I wouldn't be here. He's bleeding and needs help. He's unconscious, he could be dying!'

There was a short, startled silence, then, 'I think, miss, you're having me on. I've nothing else to do, so I can easily go and see, but before I start I know it will be a wasted journey.'

'But you will go, you promise?'

Something of her anguished urgency must have got through to the man at last. Suddenly he sounded quite disturbed. 'See here, miss—just who are you? How is it that you know all this, anyhow?'

'I—I really can't say, but I am speaking the truth.' Desperately, Julie grew threatening. 'If he bleeds to—to death it will be your responsibility. Please hurry!'

He rang off and she waited a moment, trying to pull herself together before leaving. Beating down her rising hysteria, she groaned, 'Dear heaven, let him be in time. Don't, please don't let anything happen to Brad!'

Catching a glimpse of herself in the mirrored surface of the kiosk, she gave a start of dismay. Her face was smeared by Brad's blood, which must have rubbed off her fingers, and her hair hung untidily down her shoulders. As best she could she cleaned herself up before wrapping a thin scarf tightly around her head, hoping it might effectively disguise the unhappy state she was in.

She wasn't sure how she reached home. Joe had arranged to meet Edith in town to see a show, so she had no fear of running into him, but the relief of this was offset by the struggle to catch a bus. When she did succeed the bus she caught was crowded with rain-dampened commuters. She had to stand all the way while men with a 'we're all equal now' expression on their disgruntled faces, sat. No one rose to offer her a seat.

At the cottage, Julie calculated that it was almost an hour since she had spoken to the night-watchman. Feeling torn with anxiety, she realised this wasn't enough. Soon she must ring again. By now the worst must be known; she certainly couldn't wait until morning before finding out how Brad was. It would be unbearable torture to sit here all evening, just wondering.

Yet another hour passed before she could gather enough courage to contact the night-watchman again. She heard her own sigh of relief when she managed to get hold of the same man.

'Hello,' she gulped. 'I rang some time ago about Mr Hewson. How did you find him?'

The man paused, a habit he appeared to indulge. 'In one hell of a temper, miss,' he replied dryly, 'if you'll excuse the language.'

'He was conscious?' Far from being upset by the man's language, Julie felt wild with relief.

'You can say that again!' another pause. 'Only just, mind you, but he soon made up for it.'

'His head?'

'Well, being Mr Hewson, miss, he reckons he'll live, but I advised him to let the doc have a look at him. I know I would.'

'Did he get home all right?'

'Took him there myself, miss. His man drove me back.'

A brief silence, in which Julie felt too unnerved to put the telephone down.

The man then went on, she wasn't sure whether he sounded threatening or cajoling, 'Look here, miss, could I have your name? I mean, this is all highly irregular, and you seem to know a lot about what's been going on.'

'No!' she cried in alarm, then was ashamed of thinking him too curious. 'I mean, it wouldn't do any good, would it, but I am grateful. Thank you.'

Julie wondered why she spent the next few minutes sobbing, in total anguish, when she was relieved that Brad was going to be all right. The night-watchman had said so and there was no reason why she shouldn't believe him. She must merely be suffering from reaction.

Dragging herself from the chair she had dropped into, she forced herself to make a strong cup of coffee. After drinking it she did feel a little better. Other men might have succumbed to a lesser blow than she had dealt Brad, but she might have guessed he was tough enough to get up and walk away. Tomorrow he would probably be going around as if nothing had happened! She would be the one left with the permanent damage. Would she, she wondered bitterly, always have such searing pain in her heart?

Having concentrated, until now, on Brad's recovery, Julie had almost forgotten to consider her own part in the affair. When she did pause to think of it, she found herself wondering anxiously what he might do regarding herself. Eventually she reached the unhappy conclusion that in future he would most likely ignore her. Nothing, surely, could have been more final than that last scene in his office. In an ordinary way she doubted if she would ever have seen him again, but as they both lived in the same village this might be impossible.

Again she found herself thinking of finding a job in London, once Joe married. Anything would be safer than staying too near Brad, and in London she might find it easier to forget him. She didn't stop to wonder why she thought she would have any difficulty in doing so.

Still incredibly shaken by their encounter that evening and its devastating outcome, she found it almost impossible to stop thinking of Brad. He might, she conceded, have only been trying to frighten her into agreeing to do as he asked, but the way he had chosen had surely been dangerous. If she hadn't inadvertently hit him, how long might it have been before control had gone completely? How long before they had both been overwhelmed by the force of their feelings? It could only have been moments!

Next morning Julie wasn't really surprised that she still felt terrible. Staring at herself in the mirror, she knew she looked it too. Her eyes were huge and shadowed, darkened with strain. Dismay swept her as she noticed the bruises on her neck, from the pressure of Brad's mouth as he had kissed her. Her mouth was also bruised and swollen, from the savage passion of his. Wearily regarding her reflection, she wondered if there was anything she could do about it.

In the bathroom she ran a warm bath, hoping, without much optimism, that this would repair the damage. She would have loved a hot bath, but the ancient plumbing system was rarely capable of such a thing, certainly not in the mornings.

After getting dressed she tied a silk scarf around her neck and used a lot of make-up, hoping, with any luck, that no one would notice anything unusual. She felt ill enough to have taken the day off, but it wouldn't do to stay away from work. If Brad hadn't recovered sufficiently to get to the office, and she was away as well, it might only cause unnecessary speculation.

Downstairs, Joe yawned, stretching his arms behind his head. 'Gosh,' he laughed ruefully, 'am I tired! We had a great time last night, child, but I sometimes think I'm getting too old for this kind of thing.'

'What did you do?' Julie asked, knowing it was expected of her.

'Had dinner, then saw that new show down town. Then we went out to the country and danced. We found a good spot a few miles from Repton. I must admit the food was very good, but it was late when we got back. I don't think I've managed a couple of hours' sleep.'

Where, Julie wondered, was all the money coming from? Dutifully she pushed this thought aside and smiled.

'I just hope,' Joe drowned another yawn in black coffee, 'I just hope the boss's in a better mood, this morning, than he's been in lately.'

Julie snatched up her coat, her heart racing. 'If you don't hurry, Joe, you're going to be late, and that won't help for a start.'

No one appeared to notice Julie looked far from well. Only Miss Harrison, glancing at her sharply as she passed her desk, asked if anything was wrong. Her face whitening in a way which clearly proclaimed something was, Julie shook her head, swiftly denying it and saying she felt fine. She was relieved when Miss Harrison, after a slight pause, merely nodded and let her go.

Try as she might to stop thinking of him, all morning Julie had Brad on her mind. It wasn't only the loss of his friendship, which she had been resigned to even before the fiasco in his office, it was because of the pain he might be suffering from his head, for which she felt wholly responsible. Whatever had made her pick up that table-lamp and hit him so fiercely? She knew the old saying about it being easy to be sorry afterwards, but she was filled with a terrible remorse. She knew also a strange longing, a vague wish that she might have been in the position to nurse him better. It was, she supposed, her maternal instincts coming out. Brad was an unusually dominant man and used to being in the peak of condition. The thought of him being weak and helpless, if only for a short time, appalled her. However, she told herself severely, it was no good harbouring any desire to look after him. After this he wouldn't want her anywhere near him!

It made Julie tremble to think that if she hadn't knocked him unconscious, she and Brad might have been lovers this morning. How, she wondered, would she have felt? In spite of her strict upbringing and firmly held moral standards, she was startled by the excitement which curled through her heart and stomach. Brad, she was sure, would be a very accomplished lover, and instinctively she guessed that, while he chose to give her his undivided attention, no woman would bother to look elsewhere. Or very few would, anyway. In his arms a woman might be lost for ever. With feverish truthfulness, Julie owned it, and grew even more despondent on realising that, in future, she wouldn't be seeing him again, unless it was to be severely reprimanded!

This seemed more unlikely, as the morning wore on. There was no news from Brad's office, certainly no news of him—and this, in a way, was a greater punishment than anything else. Julie's nerves became strained to breaking point, so she was scarcely aware of what she was doing. Never had she been so relieved to find her lunch hour had arrived. She wasn't hungry, but she longed for a cup of coffee. It might be better to have something, if she wasn't to break down altogether.

Deciding to go to a small café she knew, rather than face the canteen and the possibility of someone asking why she wasn't eating, Julie hurried along to the entrance. Turning a corner, she almost crashed into Brad's secretary talking to Margery Brown and Miss Harrison. With a weak smile and quick word of apology, she stepped back and around them, convinced she only imagined they looked at her in the most peculiar way.

Returning to the office, a little later, she felt surprised at the unusual volume of conversation. The cloakroom was entered from a door on the outside corridor, while another door led out of it straight into the office. Julie knew no one had seen her come in, as she was a few minutes late. She hoped Miss Harrison wasn't going to be cross. Miss Harrison was a dedicated minute-counter.

Tearing off her coat, Julie was just running a quick comb through her hair when she heard them.

'Poor man,' said Margery Brown. 'Yes, plaster and the most gorgeous black eye—and a temper to match! Of course his secretary is keeping her mouth shut! Old Harry and I couldn't get anything out of her, but she couldn't deny it, for he's making no attempt to hide it! I mean, he couldn't, could he, seeing that he's been here all morning?'

Clenching her hands tight, Julie listened numbly, as Margery continued, 'No, dear. No one is quite sure how it happened.'

'Someone must know?'

'Yes, naturally there's talk. Some say he crashed over something in the dark, but Jim Holt, the night-watchman, you know, on duty, is supposed to have told his nephew that ...'

Suddenly, as if coming to life, Julie thrust open the door, aware of an immediate silence, as many heads turned towards her. Almost she stumbled back the way she had come, thinking they must have discovered the role she had played in Brad's accident. But it was Miss Harrison's sudden appearance behind her that had apparently startled them, causing a quick return to work.

Feeling irrationally grateful, Julie said meekly to her supervisor that she was sorry for being late and went to her desk.

Brad was back at work, so he must have recovered, even if he had to bear some outward scars for a day or two. Feverishly she uttered a grateful prayer under her breath while furtively brushing an unexpected tear from her eye. She didn't notice several of the girls glancing at her curiously.

CHAPTER FOUR

THAT evening Julie went home feeling almost as dreadful as she had felt the night before. No more had been said in the office about Brad's misadventure, or if there had been she hadn't heard it, but this didn't stop her from feeling intensely unhappy about the whole thing.

Joe, surprisingly, said very little. In fact he didn't even mention it for two more days which, if she hadn't been worrying so much, Julie might have found strange. He was getting ready to go out after dinner when he remarked that Brad seemed to have had a slight accident but wasn't saying much about it. Had Julie any idea what had happened?

'I haven't seen much of him this week,' she stammered evasively.

'Not seen him?' Joe flashed her a frowning glance, as if this bothered him faintly. 'You haven't fallen out?'

Another time, Julie might have found his slightly old-fashioned phraseology amusing, especially when applied to Brad. She made herself laugh lightly. 'Good gracious, Joe, we aren't such good friends as all that. I expect I'll see him some time, when he's better.'

Joe looked relieved but still agitated. 'I see. It might be a kindness to ring him up and ask how he is. Couldn't do any harm, anyway.'

'I—I'll see.'

'Just as long as you do.'

Without pausing to consider why this seemed important to her stepfather, Julie changed the subject abruptly. 'I suppose you're getting ready to see Edith?'

'Not tonight, child,' he replied absently, glancing quickly at his wrist-watch. 'I have some—er—business to attend to, I'm afraid.'

Because she wasn't herself, Julie felt no curiosity. She simply concluded that it was probably something to do with his forthcoming marriage, or else he was going back to the works for an hour or two, something he occasionally did when they were busy.

Julie could never recall a week passing so slowly, or known one so full of strain. As each day went by she expected something terrible to happen. That nothing did, didn't seem to help one bit, it only made her apprehension much worse. Saturday, when she didn't have to go to work, was like the proverbial light at the end of a tunnel, yet when it arrived she was torn between the relief of not being in any danger of seeing Brad, and the emptiness of two whole days to devote to no one but herself.

Even so, when Rodney's mother rang asking her to dinner, so they could discuss her November the fifth party, she hesitated. Saturday evening at the Old Hall, as the Greens' small estate was called, wasn't always just family. Both Mr and Mrs Green enjoyed their friends and liked entertaining. Somehow, tonight, Julie didn't feel like facing a lot of people.

As she hesitated, Mrs Green said quickly, 'There won't be many guests tonight, dear, and I thought it would be a good opportunity. Time's getting on and I've found it difficult to get hold of you lately. As Rodney's in London I thought you might be wondering what to do with yourself.'

'I'm sorry,' Julie murmured automatically, meaning about Mrs Green not being able to get hold of her.

She was startled when Mrs Green cut in briskly, 'I know you are, dear, but he might be back soon. Seven-thirty, then. Sharp.'

Julie frowned as Mrs Green rang off. Was Rodney's mother merely jumping to conclusions, or had Rodney really given the impression that he and Julie were something more than just good friends? Julie hoped not, but for the moment there seemed little she could do about it.

Ever since Julie could remember Mrs Green had taken

a particular interest in her. Julie's father had been Mr Green's solicitor and one of his closest friends, but Julie wasn't sure that they approved of Joe. They never said anything, but she had noticed he wasn't often invited to the Old Hall, and she wondered what they thought of his coming alliance with Edith. They would probably think Edith too good for him, she thought wryly.

Julie had forgotten when she had first begun actively helping with Mrs Green's November the fifth party, which wasn't really a fireworks party, in the strictest sense of the word. They did have a small display, but most of the time was devoted to picnicking around a huge bonfire and dancing. The huge old ballroom in the house came in handy if it began raining, not an unusual occurrence in November. Tickets were sold on the basis of people giving what they liked, the proceeds of which were immediately passed on to charity. Last year they had made over a thousand pounds. Mrs Green didn't have many helpers apart from her staff, her family and Julie; she believed in keeping it simple.

Why was Rodney in London? Running upstairs, Julie suddenly realised she hadn't seen him around. It must be incredibly easy, when one's mind was so full of another man, not to notice a good friend was missing, and she felt somehow ashamed. And, now that she came to think about it, it seemed strange that Rodney had never mentioned going.

Absently she dressed, her thoughts going around in their familiar tortured circles, returning to Brad Hewson. Could he have had anything to do with Rodney's sudden departure? She doubted it, Brad hadn't been that deeply involved.

Painfully she swallowed, the whole of her suddenly longing for Brad in the most humiliating way. She wished she had been dressing to go out with him. There was no denying he had been the ideal companion. While domineering, he was also fastidious, and had known how to make her feel as though she were the most beautiful girl in the world. It was as if he had studied her moods and known what sort of evening would suit her best. Like a hunter studying his prey, she decided bitterly, while he wondered how soon he would be able to devour her!

The dress she chose suited her present mood, she thought. It was in soft, muted shades of various colours with blue predominating. The classic design enhanced the rounded curves of her slim figure, accentuating a beautifully small waist, but Julie only saw that it looked rather dull. A month ago she had purchased it in haste and never worn it. She was glad of it now, as it didn't remind her of Brad.

As she didn't drive, Mrs Green, when she asked Julie to dinner, always sent a car for her. Julie, hearing it arrive, snatched up her old velvet cape. She remembered Brad commenting, only a week or two ago, that she needed furs. All of which a man might expect to be paid for!

Mrs Green came fluttering from the kitchen, looking as though she'd been having words with her cook. 'I'm so glad you decided to come, dear,' she kissed Julie's cheek rather reproachfully. 'You haven't been to see me for ages!'

A small, rueful smile on her lips, Julie apologised, 'I'm truly sorry.' Impulsively she added, 'I think it's the way I've been feeling lately.'

Mrs Green sighed. 'I'd be willing to accept all the uncertain feelings if I could be your age again, but you've always been too sensitive, child.' Her eyes sharpened on Julie's pale face. 'There's nothing actually wrong, is there, dear?'

'No, of course not.'

More absorbed with her cook's tantrums, Mrs Green was easily deceived. Sweeping Julie into the drawing room, she left her talking to a much older mutual friend while she returned to the kitchen. Julie's companion held forth at length on the problems of present-day staff and what one was forced to put up with. Julie listened politely, glad she wasn't expected, apparently, to contribute on a topic she knew practically nothing about.

Mr Green brought them each a sherry, staying to exchange a word or two before returning to his other guests, just as his wife came back to say dinner was ready. Then, to Julie's stunned dismay, Brad Hewson arrived, with a lady.

That was how the girl clinging to his arm struck Julie —poised, elegant, altogether a superior being, like most of his women friends. She wasn't sure if it was their obvious closeness or simply the sight of Brad himself, which made her feel violently ill.

'Ah, Viola—Mr Hewson,' Mrs Green rushed forward, 'I had almost given you up!'

Feeling herself growing even colder, Julie shrank deeper in her corner, wishing she could quietly disappear. How could Mrs Green have asked them?—yet she couldn't have known.

Everyone was crowding in the doorway. Julie, bringing up the rear, heard the stranger being introduced as Viola Gardner, a distant cousin of Mrs Green's. Julie was relieved that she appeared to have been temporarily forgotten. Although she was aware that Brad must see her before many more minutes had passed, she was grateful that no one called his immediate attention to her.

After her first fleeting glance, which had been too swift to absorb much detail, Julie didn't look at him again, but she could hear Viola Gardner's bright, sophisticated chatter. Viola was the type whose beauty and self-confidence allowed her to get away with the most outrageous remarks. Clenching her tense fingers even tighter, Julie wished she could find the courage to go straight home. She had no idea, at all, how she was going to get through the rest of the evening.

At dinner, she concluded, by means of furtive deduction, that Brad must be sitting almost directly opposite her across the table. As she heard his deep voice, her heart beat unevenly. It wasn't fair, she told herself miserably, that no matter what she did she couldn't seem to get away from him! Feeling as though the world was slowly dissolving, and she with it, she tried to concentrate on the excellent soup. These days Mrs Green kept her dinner parties simple, a menu of three courses followed by cheese and coffee, but Julie found it difficult to eat anything. How much longer, she wondered, before Brad threw at her some jeering remark? He was an expert at subtleties, well able to conceal the cutting insult which only she would understand. Her nerves growing tighter by the minute, she waited.

The conversation was general, not touching on serious topics, which Mrs Green maintained caused indigestion so were best left alone at such times as this. Brad, although far from silent, continued to ignore Julie, while his voice seemed to strum through her body as if he had her heart on strings. Bitterly she realised there was nothing in his light, intelligent conversation to suggest he was enduring any of the torture she found herself subjected to.

Mrs Green, from two places away, noticed, unfortunately, that Julie wasn't eating, 'Come along, Julie dear!' she had the kind of brisk, fussy manner which drew immediate attention. 'I hope you aren't doing any of this foolish slimming? You're slim enough as it is.'

With a flush, made brilliantly obvious because of the paleness of her face, Julie shook her head. 'No, I'm sorry, Mrs Green. I—I must have been thinking of your—I mean the fireworks party.'

'Oh, we can worry about that afterwards, dear.' With a brisk, kindly smile for a girl she was fond of, Mrs Green turned again to her neighbour.

As she pushed a portion of ice-cream around her plate, to Julie's horror she felt her fork grow still as her eyes seemed slowly dragged over the table. She saw one of Brad's hands, lean and well shaped, lying on the table beside his empty plate. His shirt had a faint stripe, and was immaculate under a superb jacket which fitted his broad shoulders like a glove. His chin had a faint darkness which caused her to shiver as she recalled the slight roughness of it against her own. His mouth, this too she had known, all the sensuous ruthlessness of it.

Here she paused, knowing she was trembling but drawn by an urge much stronger than her present level of common sense. If she were quick ...? Viola was speaking to him, he was bound to be looking at her. Her hands gripping white on her spoon, Julie flashed a swift glance to his brow, never dreaming, that on her way there she would be trapped by a stare of such directness that she was unable to look away.

Her blue eyes flickered. She received the hazy impression he was pale, his face slightly haggard, but this wasn't surprising. It must have taken a lot out of him to have suffered such an attack and gone on working, as if nothing had happened.

But it was the darkness in his eyes as he stared at her that shattered her composure almost completely, and, as if to make sure she wouldn't imagine his contempt was for someone else, he said smoothly, 'Good evening, Miss Gray.'

All Julie could manage, after a moment's numb silence, was a nervous twist of her lips which she hoped, if anyone was watching, would pass for a smile.

Mrs Green, sharply attentive, exclaimed, as if she had only just realised, 'Of course! I should have remembered. Rodney told me. Julie works for you, Mr Hewson.'

'Yes.'

Mrs Green, happily unaware of anything malevolent in the briefness of Brad's reply, said warmly, 'I hope you appreciate your good luck. We all love Julie. She and Rodney are very good friends.'

Julie, as Brad was forced to give Mrs Green his attention, found herself puzzled. She felt, somehow, that Mrs Green knew more than was apparent from her seemingly guileless remarks. Surely she couldn't have asked Brad here to-

night in order to hint that she wouldn't mind having Julie
Gray for her daughter-in-law? Whatever her motive, Mrs
Green must now be fully aware that Brad had nothing but
contempt for Julie!

Coffee was served in the drawing room. Decidedly
shaken, Julie sat as far as possible from Brad, trying to
ignore him but finding herself straining to hear what he was
saying. She couldn't bear to see him so near another
woman, and wondered why this should hurt so much.
After all, he had given her the chance of going to live with
him. It was not surprising, when she refused, that he was
looking for someone else to provide the amorous pleasures
he was obviously looking for. Why then should the thought
of him making love with the girl beside him—a girl who
was clearly relishing the feel of his arm laid lightly around
her shoulders—bring nothing but pain? Yet the pain persisted, along with fear and a frightening unhappiness, and
she dared not even glance at him for fear of giving herself
away.

Not sure what she was so terrified of betraying, Julie
could feel nerves gathering in tight knots in her stomach.
Her face felt tight, too, and after forcing her coffee down
she felt sick. Hoping no one would notice, she sneaked out,
running frantically upstairs. This time her sickness wasn't
imagined and she was wretchedly grateful there was no one
around. The servants had gone to their quarters, now that
dinner was over, and this part of the house was quiet.
Coming out at last, after rinsing her face and mouth, she
almost fell over Brad, propped against the bathroom door.

'Oh!' she gasped, her face like paper, her eyes huge
with shocked surprise. 'What are you doing here?'

'Men have the same needs as women,' he rejoined sarcastically.

'Yes,' she whispered, without realising what she was
saying. Unable to restrain herself any longer, her eyes flew
to his face. Above his right eye, which was unflatteringly
streaked with black and yellow, was a large patch of stick-

ing plaster. He made no attempt to disguise it, his hair was well brushed back. It gave him the appearance of an old time buccaneer. Julie could imagine him fighting for his king and country, and over a woman—and winning!

Suddenly, to her horror, he grasped her shoulders, pulling her closer. As his voice cut through her thoughts harshly, his eyes leapt with anger.

'Go on, take a good look at all the damage you've done! Like all women you like to gloat.'

'No ...!' White to the lips, she shrank back from him, covering her face with her hands.

These he jerked quickly away while one of his fingers ripped the plaster from his brow. Under it lay an ugly wound which was healing but which still looked sore and red.

As Julie stared at it, aghast to realise the strength she must have used to cause a cut of such depth, he jeered, 'It warranted three or four stitches, you'll be pleased to hear.'

'No—Brad ...'

He paused significantly, his eyes glittering narrowly, 'You didn't know what you were doing, I suppose, when you lashed out at me with a table-lamp?'

'No,' she half sobbed, 'I didn't!'

'I thought as much.'

Too late she understood the trap into which she had so stupidly fallen. 'You had me frightened, almost out of my mind.'

'Oh I had you out of your mind, all right, but not with fright. If there was any fright it was because of your own reactions. You wanted me to make love to you. You wanted me to go the whole way. You won't ever convince me otherwise. I could feel it.'

This frightened her, his terrible astuteness, but she had to deny it. 'It helps your pride to believe it.'

A grunt of derision escaped his tight mouth. 'I like your body better than I like you. At least it doesn't lie.'

The darkness of his eyes was so unrelenting she had to close her own eyes against it. Under her breath she found she was uttering a silent prayer. 'I did my best, Brad. I sent someone to look after you.'

'Instead of keeping your head and waiting until I came round yourself. Then I could have got home without anyone being any the wiser.'

What he didn't point out was perfectly clear. 'I'm sorry,' she whispered, 'if you feel there's been undue publicity, but you could be mistaken. I haven't heard anything. Maybe I should have acted differently, but I could see you had to have help. You might have died!'

'Would you have cared?'

This time she couldn't answer, it was pride which at last forced her to shake her head.

'Liar!' he retorted, his voice still vibrating with scorn and anger.

'I'm not!' Some of her courage returning, Julie almost hissed at him.

Suddenly Brad took hold of her, thrusting her back into the bathroom and closing the door.

'Go on, shout!' he taunted, as Julie opened her mouth.

Fright and the familiar excitement whirled through her as she realised he had her trapped. The situation might be impossible to explain, if she cried for help and they were found. Wildly she tried other tactics, convinced Brad Hewson was just trying to frighten her. 'What's Viola going to say when she comes looking for you?'

'She wouldn't believe I was in here with you, and she's unlikely to break down the door.'

'You beast!'

He made no reply as he glanced slowly around. 'This is a nice big bathroom,' he said, taking off his jacket and hanging it behind the door.

Helplessly she stared at him, knowing it was futile to fight yet aware she mustn't give in to him. If he had had love in his heart how different it might have been. Then she might have surrendered gladly. But all she could read in his face was a ravaging desire for revenge. Hate was stamped on every part of him.

'Come here.' It was an order, contemptuously given. When she didn't move his arms reached out to drag her against his hard body. As she stared wildly up into his smouldering eyes, at the sensuous mouth so close to her own, she felt shaken by the depth of his dark desire.

Then she was stretched against the hard length of him, so she could feel the impact of each individual muscle. She had a feeling he was deliberately treating her without respect, so alive was his intent to punish.

'You'll have to think twice before telling me you don't respond after this,' Brad rasped, his fingers sliding through her hair to pull her head back.

Then everything was hurting, his hard, searching mouth which explored hers without mercy, his hands which twisted her around to him as he kissed her, so he could slide down the zip of her dress to grasp cruelly on her warm flesh.

She wanted to cry out, to hurt him as badly as he was hurting her, but suddenly she began feeling dizzy. Her limbs went weak and she was shaken by an overwhelming physical passion which demanded to be satisfied. It wasn't Brad Hewson she was fighting any more but the searing strength of her own emotions. They were becoming a tangible force as sensation passed deep within her. She heard the wind rising outside the window, but wasn't sure if it was the wind that moaned, or herself.

Someone tried the door, and Julie found herself thrust heavily away from him. 'Say you'll only be a few minutes,' he commanded harshly.

Like one in a trance she found the voice to obey and, as the footsteps receded, Brad reached for his jacket while studying her ravaged face.

'Don't think I'm satisfied yet,' he said grimly.

'You'll never get another chance,' she said fiercely, wish-

ing desperately that he didn't know her arms had been
tight around his neck. Hoping to rid him of such evidence
of weakness, she added tensely, 'I'm leaving your employment just as soon as I can, so you won't have any further
hold over me.'

'We'll see about that,' he almost snarled, leaving her so
abruptly it took her some seconds to comprehend that he
had gone.

Julie intended handing in her notice at the end of that week
and didn't think anyone, not even Brad, for all his devious
threats, could prevent her. On Saturday evening she hadn't
seen him again. On going downstairs she found he and
Viola Gardner had left. Mrs Green, who had apparently
seen them off, said that they were going on to dance somewhere. Mulling over this silently, Julie knew she ought to
be pleased, and able to forget them, but all she had seen
during the next few hours was the image of this other
girl, dancing in Brad's arms.

Even at work this picture continued to haunt her and
the planning of an exciting future in London didn't help to
get rid of it altogether. After the incident in the bathroom
at the Old Hall, which still shocked her, she didn't see
Brad again. Frequently she found herself wishing things
hadn't gone so wrong between them but there seemed
nothing that she could possibly do, about it.

It was Joe who shattered her rocking universe completely, by starting on a chain of events which had terrible
repercussions. One evening after work he was unable to
eat the excellent meal Julie had cooked, and when she
asked him what was wrong his face crumpled in the most
alarming way and he collapsed, head in hands, on the table.

Julie, who had never seen a man break down like this
before, was startled and concerned. Immediately she
thought he and Edith must have quarrelled, but apparently
this was not the case. When she asked if this was the
trouble, Joe shook his head, but then, to her utter horror,

he confessed he had embezzled a large sum of money from the firm, amounting to several hundreds of pounds.

'You can't have done!' Shaking with fright, Julie stared at him, her face white. 'Joe—you couldn't have done anything like that?'

Glancing quickly into her entreating eyes, he looked away again. His voice was hoarse. 'I'm afraid I have.'

Julie closed her eyes for a moment tightly, wondering how many times recently she had felt sick. 'I just can't believe it,' she gasped weakly. 'Oh, Joe, how could you!'

'I'm sorry, child,' he mumbled morosely.

Some people were only sorry they got found out! Julie, feeling ashamed of such a thought, tried to pull herself together. Joe was rapidly going to pieces, she must try to get some sense out of him.

'Does anyone know about this yet?' she asked urgently. 'You haven't told Brad?'

Why she thought of Brad immediately she wasn't sure, but it was his firm, and she suspected Joe had collapsed because he'd been found out. Her hopes were dashed and her horror seemed to increase when Joe nodded.

As she gazed at him speechlessly, he added, 'He's the only one who knows, so far.'

Not immediately could she find the courage to enquire what Brad was going to do. 'Why on earth should you want to steal money, Joe? You have a good salary.'

'Yes,' he agreed briefly, with a pathetic sniff, 'I suppose I did it because of Edith.'

'Edith?'

Sullenly he shrugged his stout shoulders. 'You wouldn't understand, Julie. I've always lived up to the hilt. I have no savings, no car—at least I didn't have. Then we live in a rented house and the furniture is all your mother's.'

'But I thought you were going to live with Edith?'

'I didn't know that then, did I? Even so, a chap likes to make some impression.'

'And you decided the best way to do this was by stealing! Oh, Joe ...' miserably Julie blinked away a frantic tear, 'now you'll be prosecuted. It could mean——' She couldn't find the nerve to finish.

'Prison!' Joe supplied, with an emphasis she found confusing.

At last she could put it off no longer. 'Is that what Brad says? It's a wonder he allowed you to come home? It's a wonder he didn't have you arrested right away, he's not usually so tolerant.'

'Julie!' Joe cut through her flow of words which were growing wilder. 'He didn't say what he intends doing. He wants to see you first.'

'Me?' Julie felt herself growing cold with apprehension. Was this to be Brad's revenge? Was he going to list her as an accomplice and send her to prison with Joe? How he must be congratulating himself on having got rid of her before this reached the newspapers! In asking to see her he was taking a last opportunity to crow. Eating humble pie, biting the dust—whatever one called it, it added up to utter humiliation and tragedy!

'I haven't been seeing Brad lately, Joe, you know that.'

'We know he's been like a bear with a sore head, even before he got one—which isn't like him.'

'We?' she queried.

'Everybody in the office.'

'I see. Well, he did say he hadn't had a holiday.' Julie hesitated, her voice trembling. 'Did he say why he wants to see me?'

'I'm sure I don't know.'

She frowned, unable to understand Joe's suddenly offhand manner, but perhaps, like herself, he was trying to put on a brave face. Besides, some of the fault must be hers. If she hadn't been so absorbed in her own affairs she might have noticed Joe was worried. When he had groused about not having a new car, there must have been danger signals she should have noticed.

Joe was speaking again, words which shocked her, for

she was unprepared for anything to happen immediately.

'He's coming here tonight, chick, and he told me to make myself scarce. Anyway, I promised Edith I'd be around to watch television.'

Two hours later, when Brad called, Julie was still worried sick over Joe's attitude. He seemed to have gone off to see Edith as if he had done nothing worse than take an office pencil. No—she was wrong there. His face had been grey, and, as she had helped him on with his coat, she had felt him shaking. But how he could have gone out at all, with this hanging over him, was beyond her. If it hadn't been for the sake of her dead mother, and Edith—both good women—Julie wasn't sure if she'd have been very willing to do anything to help him.

Brad Hewson knocked, and, for all she had known he was coming, the nervous fright which rushed through her on finding him on the doorstep made her wonder if she wasn't about to faint. In other circumstances, she told herself, she could have dealt with him smartly, but not now. Yet, reluctant to appear as cowardly as Joe, she made a valiant effort to straighten her slender shoulders.

'You'd better come in,' she said.

He didn't smile, either, but simply pushed past her as he stepped inside, closing the door for her. Narrowly he glanced at her, seeing the extreme paleness of her face, the huge, shadowed eyes, fixed on him, full of unconscious terror. He didn't need to guess at the ordeal she was going through.

'I'm going to help myself to a drink,' he said abruptly, as they went to the sitting room. 'You'd better have one, too.'

Julie had no patience with such trivialities. No drink, she was sure, would help her now. However, she made no protest when Brad placed one in her hand. It might be something to look at, rather than Brad's merciless face.

Sitting down, because her legs felt so weak, she realised dully that she and Brad had nothing more to say to each other. Friendship and everything else had gone. He was a stranger, not the man who had often held her in his arms and made tender love to her. She knew they had only one thing left to talk about, and she must make a start on this at once.

'What,' she asked woodenly, 'are you going to do about Joe?'

Brad drank off his whisky, then, getting rid of his glass, stood looking down at her, 'That,' he replied evenly, 'is entirely up to you.'

Blankly Julie looked at him, unable to escape the intentness of his eyes, the black mockery which seemed to be there for her alone, but this time she wasn't sure what he meant. 'Is it true,' she faltered, 'that Joe has actually stolen a lot of money?'

'Yes,' he said briefly, without a change of expression. 'But if he hadn't come to me and confessed it might have been several weeks before his theft was discovered through the usual channels.'

'How was he ever tempted to do such a thing?' She felt her cheeks go hot with shame.

Brad's mouth tightened. 'Hasn't he told you?'

'Nothing—nothing, that is, that I can understand very clearly.' Pausing, Julie found herself watching Brad very carefully, wondering how much she should say. He wasn't wearing the plaster on his forehead now, but the wound still looked red and sore. Each time he looked at it he must remember who was responsible, and this would instantly dismiss any leniency he might have felt towards Joe.

When Brad didn't speak, she tried again, with hands clenched whitely. 'I believe he wanted another car, things like that.'

'And he thought it was quite permissible to steal, in order to get it. Did you benefit as well, I wonder?'

Wildly she began to jump to her feet, only to sink back again helplessly. Suddenly she was frightened, appalled that Brad should think this of her. 'You know that's not true,' she cried huskily.

'Perhaps,' he conceded, no trace of kindness in his voice as he coolly appraised her.

'I suppose you find it impossible to believe I feel awful about this?' she choked, feeling herself shaking and knowing he could see it. It threw her into even greater turmoil to realise it must be up to her to plead for clemency for Joe, although she wasn't sure that Brad would grant it. Hating to have to beg, she drew a deep breath, trying to face him bravely. 'Would you—I mean, could you give us time to pay you back?'

Formidably Brad asked, 'How long would it take you to repay over five thousand pounds?'

'Five thousand!' Julie heard herself croaking with shock. 'He—he said hundreds ... It can't be true!'

Brad's mouth curled contemptuously. 'Obviously he forgot to mention how many. Five thousand is what he's confessed to, but it will have to be checked.'

'There could be more?' The room was going hazy.

'It's possible.'

Like a girl in a trance, Julie fixed wide, glazed eyes on him. 'If we could borrow it would be difficult to even repay the interest.'

'Exactly!' Brad's tone was menacing, it also held a note of triumph she found difficult to understand. 'And who would lend you such a sum—not forgetting it might be more, not less. Joe is only a year or two off retirement and your salary will barely keep you, especially after he marries and you'll be on your own.'

The darkness of utter despair hitting her mercilessly, Julie collapsed in a huddle. Resting her elbows on her knees, she buried her face in her hands. How could Joe have done this? It was so stupid! He must have known he would be found out, that it would cause terrible trouble!

Her breath ragged, she whispered through tense fingers, 'Why did he have to go to you? I know you're the boss, but why should he expect you to help him?'

'Because of you.'

'Because of me?' she stammered, shocked afresh. 'He must know—I told him, I hadn't been out with you lately.'

'We were friendly enough when he first started to borrow, apparently. He risked a lot on the strength of your attractions.'

Even at such a time as this, Brad's derision had the power to hurt. Bleakly she took her hands from her face. 'He must have been mad!'

'Why?'

'Well, he must have known you could have no real interest in me.'

'You sound very sure of that?'

'Brad!' Suddenly she was on her feet, facing him, almost screaming at him. 'Will you stop playing with me! You must have better things to do. Just tell me frankly, how long will it be before you go to the police?'

'Stop snivelling!' he snapped. 'I don't have to go to the police. That is,' he drawled slowly, eyes fixed uncaring on the tears streaming down her face, 'I'm quite sure I can prevent this from going any further, but only if I get the right encouragement.'

Some part of her mind shied away from this. 'He could sell his car!'

'You'd still be thousands short.'

'I see ...' Julie looked up at Brad, her eyes huge with despair. 'Well, thank you for coming to speak to me personally about it. I'll have to stand by Joe, of course, see him through. It seems about all I can do.'

'Not exactly all, Julie.'

She sighed, like someone too tired to want to bother any more. 'What do you mean, this time?'

'You'd better sit down again.' One sharp glance at her face and he was guiding her quite gently back to the settee. 'I'll get you another drink. Maybe you're going to need it.'

CHAPTER FIVE

WHEN Julie refused his offer of another drink he stood for a moment as though contemplating the degree of apprehension in her face, then with an indifferent shrug he dropped down beside her.

'Just tell me what you want me to do,' she pleaded, trying helplessly to stifle further tears. She felt tense and terribly scared, too conscious that there was little compassion in the harsh features of the man who lounged by her side like a waiting tiger.

The only sympathy he offered was in the form of a large white handkerchief which he produced unused, with an impatient gesture from his pocket.

'Here,' he said curtly, 'take this, but don't waste too many tears, not until you've refused my final offer.'

'Which is?'

'That you live with me.'

'Live—with you!' Shivering, Julie thrust the handkerchief over her eyes, around her mouth, so he shouldn't see her horrified reaction. He might have been ordering a box of matches, there was so little emotion in his voice.

'It's not something new.' His eyes locked on hers, assessing her agonised despair, dismissing it as if it counted for nothing.

'You've asked me before,' she gasped, meaning that he was wasting his time.

'I'm asking you again, for the last time.' The cold challenge in his voice made her cringe. 'Agree, and I'll promise to put back every penny Joe has taken. If not then I'm afraid there's nothing I can do.'

Julie was stricken. Her face, already pale, felt frozen as she stared at him in an agony of doubt. To live with him! Under no illusion as to what this would mean, she knew she was trapped. To begin with there might be delight, but how long would it last? Soon when he grew tired of her, would follow disillusionment and heartache. Perhaps if she got off with this she might be fortunate, but she suspected he might demand a lot more than she might want to give. If he had loved her but hadn't been free to marry, it could have been different. As it was, he was quite free to marry, but there was no love in his heart, for either her or anyone else. When he married it would be to someone like Viola Gardner, a woman with the right kind of background.

Her throat tight with strain, Julie whispered, 'Brad, I must have time before I can make up my mind. You hate me, and even if you didn't we have little in common.'

'Maybe this will help you make up your mind.'

Before she could move he put his arm around her shoulders, toppling her against him. Almost leisurely he bent his head, touching her mouth lightly, while with his free hand he slowly undid the buttons at the top of her blouse. Then gently but very sensuously his hand slid over her, until her skin burned and her heart began throbbing wildly. Within seconds, as if under some powerful sexual attack, the pulse at the base of her throat was racing out of control.

He said thickly, a nerve jerking at the side of his mouth, 'If you're playing for time, I'm not giving you any. You can decide now, even if I have to wait all night.'

Next morning, Julie moved like a girl in a trance, a nightmare, which frightened her dreadfully. She kept remembering how frail her defences had been against Brad, as he had held her. Consumed by the longing stirred by the expert stroking of his hands, all her resistance had fled. Looking at him, trying hard to conceal the desire he was arousing, she choked, 'I don't seem to have any alternative, do I?'

'No attractive alternative,' he had agreed, ruthlessly,

drawing away from her, a glint of steely satisfaction in his eyes.

Almost before she had finished tidying herself despairingly, Joe arrived. Banging shut the front door, he had rushed to the sitting room, his face that of a man hoping for a miracle. Brad had told him grimly that he could stop worrying. That he would arrange everything, he and Julie between them.

Joe, showing an amazing disinclination to know how this was to be accomplished, had been overflowing with gratitude. Effusive thanks had tumbled from him in a stream.

Brad cut through these with abrupt contempt. 'I'll see you in the office first thing in the morning. There are still some questions to be answered.'

As he made to leave immediately, his eyes had narrowed coldly on Julie's distraught face. 'I'll see you later in the day, Julie, as soon as we get through.'

Joe, when at last they were alone together, had stunned her by rubbing his hands gleefully. 'So he's actually going to overlook what I did!'

'I believe so.'

'Phew! Well, that's a relief. Thanks, Julie.'

Incredulously she had gazed at him. Never a word about trying to repay the money he had taken, not a single query as to what she had done—what she was going to have to do, to extract such a promise from Brad. She had never had any great affection for Joe, but in that moment she despised him. There were things she could have said, but she had felt too sick to utter any of them. She felt embittered against all men; that she was to be forced to live with one of them filled her with nothing but repugnance. What could be the use of sexual attraction when there was only hate in her heart?

After breakfast she was astonished that Joe appeared hurt when she refused to ride to work with him.

'Oh, come on, Julie!' he protested.

'I'm sorry, Joe,' she returned stiffly, scarcely able to prevent herself shouting that she could never bring herself to ride in a car bought with stolen money. She was glad when, as if realising what was on her mind, he drove off sullenly.

All morning, as she typed automatically, Julie tried to envisage what her future was going to be, but each time she thought of Brad her heart beat so heavily she was forced to think of something else. Waiting for him to send for her began to resemble the most refined kind of torture and her hands shook on her typewriter keys as she wondered how long it would be before he sent for her permanently.

The conviction that Brad wouldn't ask her to go through with it wasn't strong enough to be realistic. He must have been looking for revenge since she had first refused to go away with him, but after she had been foolish enough to hit him over the head, his desire to utterly humiliate her, to drag her down to the level of a kept woman must have increased threefold. Joe must have played unwittingly into his hands.

A kept woman? No, she wasn't being completely fair. Brad had said she could get a job, if she really wanted to, so this must rule out a little of that particular stigma. But she would still be doing something that went against all her personal principles. Others managed to live with it, and circumstances differed, for some it was all they would ever have, but Julie felt, at her age, there was time enough to settle for something like that. Bitterness against Brad Hewson welled in her heart, obliterating everything else.

At twelve-thirty she went up to his office. His secretary told her to go straight in, he was expecting her. Again Julie noticed the curiosity on the woman's kindly face.

Brad was sitting at his desk, as usual. When she opened the door he glanced up quickly and she recoiled, as though her courage had given way.

'Come in,' he said quietly, holding her with his intent gaze as surely as if his hands gripped her. As she came nearer, he rose to pull out a chair. 'Sit down.'

When she obeyed, he returned to his own chair behind

the desk. The afternoon sun, through the window behind him, struck directly on Julie's pale face, keeping his deviously in the shadow.

Taking one narrowed look at her haunted expression, he rang for coffee. 'I asked you to live with me,' he said between his teeth, 'not jump in the river.'

Struggling with chaotic thoughts, Julie gasped, 'Jumping in the river wouldn't worry me nearly so much. I can swim.'

'You can also learn to make love, if you don't know already,' he replied harshly. 'I think you'll find it even more enjoyable.'

Trying to hide her scarlet cheeks, she dipped her head as she retorted, 'That might be a matter of opinion. It must depend ...'

'On whom you're with? I agree,' he cut in mockingly. 'But so far as you and I are concerned, I think you can rid yourself of any doubts.'

His secretary brought their coffee, but he didn't ask Julie to pour. He saw to the task himself, as if demonstrating that he was only letting her into his life so far.

'What is it you want me to do?' she asked, trying to summon the last vestige of pride as she lifted her head. How did a man manage to appear so tough and formidable yet so smoothly elegant at the same time? There was a strength about him which could never be disputed, but a determination to have his own way which made her shudder.

'What do I want you to do?' she heard him repeating, a taunting smile on his mouth. 'I'm afraid you'll find that out soon enough, but to begin with you could look a bit more cheerful.'

'I'll try,' she shivered sharply, restraining an urgent desire to get up and run.

'Then try harder,' he ground out.

When she made no reply but lifted her cup with shaking fingers, he gave an exasperated sigh. 'I've been sorting things out with Joe. I hate to tell you he's a thief and a scoundrel, who certainly deserves time for what he's done.'

'Can you ...' Her voice cracked and she made small despairing movements with her hands. She hated the term while feeling forced to use it. 'Can you—hush it up?'

'I believe so.' He held her gaze, his eyes dark on her frozen face. 'This doesn't let you out. One word from me ...'

'I don't go back on my promises, Brad.'

'You'd better not!'

The threat in his voice was soft but wholly frightening. Before her control snapped altogether, Julie dug her nails into the soft palms of her hands and cleared her throat huskily. 'Hadn't you better stop threatening me and tell me what happens next?'

'All in good time.' Getting up, with a grim smile, he came around to where she sat and drew her to her feet, while she stared up at him with pain-filled eyes.

She trembled as he touched her. This near she was too aware of the cut on his forehead, just as she was also aware that in this room it had all happened. As soon as she had come here today, her eyes had been drawn to the low unit, where she had left him bleeding helplessly. How different her thoughts had been then!

Staring down at her slim figure, Brad appeared to be studying her neat black skirt and white blouse without notable favour. Deliberately, holding her firmly, he drew the pins from her hair until it fell in a thick, shining swathe down her back.

'That's better,' he said softly. 'Like that, you even begin to look worth a few thousand pounds.'

High tension leapt through her body, hitting her heart with a force which nearly stopped the blood runing. 'Whatever that money buys,' she cried wildly, 'it won't be my love. I hate you!'

'You didn't exactly hate me the last time I touched you,' he rejoined calmly. 'But a little hate can add spice.'

As though to demonstrate his point, he drew her slowly to him, inexorably closing the space between their lips as

if he already owned her. There was an instant flare of reaction to tighten his grasp. For an agonised moment she
tried to resist him, but couldn't. From a density of smouldering smoke there seemed to leap wild flames of desire.
His hands burned her shoulders and she felt weak, unable
to battle against the emotion within her while knowing she
must.

Lifting his head, Brad caught something of her abject
despair and waited for the knowledge of her own vulner-
ability to sink in. 'You're getting quite a bargain, Julie,'
he said coolly. 'It might help if you think of it this way.'

Shrinking from his callous tones, she longed to hurt him
as he was hurting her. 'What about yourself, do you believe
you're getting a bargain too? Do you really believe I'm
worth all that money?'

He smiled tightly. 'If you're not now, you're going to be.
I'll make very sure of that.' He touched her hot cheek,
pushed her hair back while his eyes roamed over her
frankly. Suddenly he seemed to relax and his smile softened.
'You might feel cornered, Julie Gray, but I assure you that
in a few weeks' time you'll feel very different. Meanwhile,
all I ask is that you'll be ready to come with me, when I
want you.'

Numbly she tried to beat down the wave of fear this
aroused. Blue eyes trapped by his darker ones, she asked
apprehensively, 'How—how long?'

Firmly he sat her down again. 'I should be through
here in a few days, a week at the most, then we go off together, you and I, somewhere where no one will know
us. Not because of any wish on my part to hide you, but
because I want you to myself for quite a time. You attract
me very much, my dear.'

'Brad, please,' suddenly desperate, she knew she must
plead with him, 'does it have to be like this?'

Hope died as she saw he didn't intend yielding an inch.
His voice was low, without harshness, but very determined,
'You surely don't believe I would be cruel, do you, my

dear? I think I know why you're frightened. You haven't had an affair with a man before. But there has to be a first time, you know, and I promise I'll be gentle.'

Panic made Julie's heart flutter like that of a trapped wild bird. Was that supposed to be comforting? But she had to steel herself to ignore the odd note of persuasion in his voice. How easy, if she had no regard for right or wrong, to give in to him. This she must never do. Somehow she must find a way out!

'What happens when we come home?' she tried to sound as though she didn't much care.

He raised his dark brows, sardonically. 'I thought I told you I'll get you a flat, anywhere you like in London, and, if you want it, some work as well. I'm not keen on having you working. I'd rather you kept your energy for me, but if you insist.'

'I—I don't know . . .'

'We don't have to discuss it just now, Julie.'

Another problem occurred to her, just one more in what seemed a ghastly parade of them. 'What will I tell Joe?'

A frown marked Brad Hewson's brow. 'I suppose you have to tell him something, or you feel you have to, but I don't think he'll demand an explanation. He's not in a position to start throwing his weight around. If I were you I'd just say I was getting a job in London and leave it at that. He has his fiancée to look after him.'

'Yes, I expect they'll soon be married.' Somehow Julie couldn't keep a trace of bitterness from her voice.

She didn't notice his suddenly watchful glance on her white face, but she did hear his taunting laugh. 'So you envy him that? I'd advise you to concentrate instead on how I'm going to spoil you. If you're prepared to meet me halfway, my dear, you won't regret it. You'll have a far better time living with a man than being married to him.'

Feeling it would be useless to comment on that, she asked hopelessly, 'Will you introduce me to your friends?'

He replied smoothly, 'We'll have to see.'

Fiercely she glared at him, her slight body stiff with resentment. Not sure whether to laugh or cry, she said bleakly, 'You sound like a man who's done it all before.'

Any tolerance on his face disappeared. 'Few men reach my age, Julie, without having spent the odd night with a woman, the occasional weekend even, but I've never gone as far as this before. Does that answer your question?'

'I ...'

'Look, Julie,' he cut in harshly, 'let's leave it. This isn't going to get us anywhere. I suggest you stop asking questions which I don't particularly want to answer, and leave everything to me.'

When she got home that evening Julie wasn't surprised to find a note from Joe saying he had gone to see Edith and wasn't sure what time he would be back. Joe was obviously embarrassed and avoiding his stepdaughter. Somehow Julie fancied she wouldn't be seeing much of him from now on. He wouldn't want to know what she had had to do to get him out of his fix, just as long as he got off scot free. Brad was right, she realised bitterly, in implying that Joe was only concerned for himself.

All the same, she wished there had been someone here to talk to. Someone who might have taken her mind off her own problems instead of leaving it to veer wildly between the incredible excitement she found in Brad's arms and the total rejection she found inside her for the kind of life he was planning they should live together.

How different it might have been had they been engaged —like Edith and Joe. Then she might have been able to enjoy some of the privileges of a fiancée. While Brad had arranged to take her to lunch tomorrow, he hadn't offered to bring her home tonight. Nor had he appeared to worry that she must struggle for a bus in a typical November downpour. Such casual treatment she evidently must get used to, unless, she thought desperately, removing her wet coat, she could think of something to make Brad change his mind.

For lunch with Brad she didn't think of wearing anything but her usual office blouse and skirt, which she found him eyeing disparagingly as they sat down in one of the city's best restaurants.

'You'll need some new clothes.'

Faint colour touched her cheeks as she glanced uncertainly across at him. 'I—I hadn't thought of it, but I can get one or two things.'

'I'll buy you plenty when we get to Paris, but it could be a day or two before we feel like doing any shopping.'

Her eyes widened on his, and with a flickering alarm she felt the colour in her face deepen swiftly. He was staring at her, his eyes very sober, but something smouldered in their depth, making her suddenly tremble. 'Paris?' she repeated, stupidly. The name for Julie had always possessed a certain magic, but she hadn't thought of Brad taking her there.

'Why not?' his voice lowered mockingly. 'It can be a wonderful place for lovers.'

'Of—of course, you would know all about that!'

'I didn't say that,' the cleft in his square chin seemed to be chiselled from iron. 'If you're trying hard to please me, my dear child, I can still see room for improvement.'

She trembled, hating his sarcasm, not ready to agree that his complaint was justified. 'A relationship,' in spite of trying to speak bravely she had to swallow twice, 'a relationship such as ours is going to be doesn't burden me with the obligations of a wife.'

'I wondered when you'd get around to that.' One of her hands lay on the table. As he took hold of it, his grip tightened cruelly. 'As far as obligations go don't forget you haven't paid anything yet, and I'm not running a charity. You owe me plenty.'

Her blue eyes merged with his until she felt burnt. 'You love to remind me!'

'You leave me no other choice.'

'You—you're ...'

'Don't say it,' he snapped, 'or you might easily find yourself visiting Joe in one of Her Majesty's prisons, instead of wandering with me along the boulevards of Paris.'

Prison! The word haunted Julie. For Joe's sake she dare not go too far. Brad wasn't a man to indulge in idle threats. She bit her beautifully curved lower lip nervously.

His eyes followed the agitated movement of her perfect white teeth with interest. 'About these clothes,' he drawled.

'I'll buy something myself.'

'Off the cheapest peg you can find?'

Her blue eyes sparkled frostily, with a defiance which narrowed his thoughtfully. 'It's a wonder you've ever taken me out, when you think my clothes so awful!'

'The only thing wrong with your clothes, my dear, is that every other girl appears to be wearing the same thing. A face and figure like yours deserves something more exclusive. Only the best.'

Julie hated that her heart jerked, at what she considered was insincere flattery. He wouldn't have asked her to go away with him if he hadn't thought her attractive but she had little doubt that revenge was the stronger motive. Revenge that she had refused him, in the first place, then hit him over his head, then because of Joe.

Mechanically she said, 'I'm sorry about my clothes, but they're the best I can manage.'

'On your salary, I agree, but your life style is going to be rather different.'

That she choked on her soup made her exclaim quite untruthfully, 'I've seen some very shabby mistresses.'

'Be quiet!'

Once she had had the audacity to strike him, even if it had been unintentional. Now she feared, as his anger leapt, that he was going to hit her back.

As she shrank from him instinctively, undisguised terror in her eyes, he said savagely, 'Don't worry, I can think of better ways than that. There are much more refined methods of quietening people than with a lamp.'

'I—I hate you, Brad Hewson!'

'And that's something else I don't want to hear again, not unless you mean it.'

About to continue her wild defiance, she found something in his face warned her to think again. A shiver of fright caught her so she was unable to speak. His eyes were going slowly over her, slipping across her breast, caressing her neck, the long line of her throat, finishing on the full, sensuous curves of her mouth. The shiver inside her deepened.

'Are you willing yet to talk sensibly about your wardrobe?' he asked with exaggerated politeness.

Eventually he allowed that she should go herself to purchase enough to see her through their first few days in Paris. Julie pleaded that while she wasn't well known, he was, and to accompany her to the best shops in the city would only cause unnecessary gossip. Afterwards she wondered why he had agreed to spare her the humiliation of having him personally pay for her clothes. It was bad enough having to accept the huge wad of notes he thrust coolly into her shabby handbag, without a shred of pity for the surge of pink which coloured her pallid cheeks.

'Only buy models,' he ordered curtly, 'and,' he added deliberately, looking full at her, 'if you dare come back with serviceable underwear, I'll throw the whole lot out and buy the next lot myself!'

After lunch, so that she could go shopping, he gave her the afternoon off, saying he would inform her office. While he was busy, he said, he would also tell Miss Harrison that Julie would be leaving at the end of the week, just so there could be no mistake. As he left her, Julie couldn't help wondering what Miss Harrison was going to make of that. Not for the first time she wished she could just quietly disappear!

In an ordinary way, if she had had as much to spend as

she had now, Julie might have enjoyed herself. As it was she made her purchases quickly, relying on her unerring good taste. She brought two day dresses, two evening ones and a warm velvet cloak that felt like silk. Brad had insisted he would buy her a fur coat in London, before they left. In a daze she bought shoes and gloves and handbags, leaving the lingerie until last.

Something came over her blindly as she surveyed the piles of diaphanous negligees, the filmy nightdresses, the scanty bras and panties, all frothed with foaming lace. Without seeming to draw breath she bought at random, bras which consisted of mere scraps of transparent silky lace, panties so brief they scarcely seemed to exist, nightdresses of the finest silks and satins, beautiful creations of such fragile material it would seem almost a shame to wear them. Especially when she shivered to think of what they might suffer beneath a man's rough hands!

As Brad had ordered she took a taxi home, her packages piled in the back. Since she had bought all her things from the one exclusive store, this had been easy enough, but by the time she reached home she felt exhausted. The telephone was ringing when she got in. It was Joe.

'I've been trying to get hold of you,' he said. 'I'm having to sort a few things out with Brad, but tomorrow night Edith has asked me to go to Grantham with her to meet her sister. She would like to stay overnight and I'm just wondering if you could pack me a case. It could be midnight before I get back tonight and there's never time to spare in the mornings.'

When Julie promised woodenly to do her best, he added quickly, 'You'd better put in an extra shirt. If I can get the day after tomorrow off, Edith and I might stay longer.'

Amazed, Julie gathered up her parcels and stumbled upstairs. Joe had sounded rather muddled, but how he could be contemplating going off at all, after what he had done, was beyond her.

Joe's wasn't the only call she had that evening. Rodney

Green rang while she was sitting quietly weeping, bowed down under a weight of despair. When she heard the telephone she thought it might be Brad and made a great effort to dry her eyes and control her voice.

'Julie Gray,' she began, then, 'Why, Rodney! I didn't know you were home again.'

'I'm not,' he laughed, 'I'm still in London, but I'll be home tomorrow night. You haven't forgotten our party?'

'Oh, Rodney,' she wasn't sure what to say, 'I've been busy. Your mother was in touch, but this year she's got plenty of helpers. I really don't know if I can go.'

'What?' His indignation came over loud and clear. 'I asked you weeks ago, Julie. You promised!'

'Yes.' Guilt flooded her as she tried unhappily to think of an excuse. How could she explain her changed circumstances to Rodney, or anyone? She hadn't the courage to confess that she was going to live with Brad Hewson, especially when she could never tell Rodney about Joe. Brad, of course, would never agree to her going to the party without him. 'I don't think I would be much fun to take anywhere at the moment,' she ended lamely.

Refusing to believe it, Rodney swept this aside. 'Tell you what, Julie darling, I'll pick you up at seven thirty sharp. I'll come myself, and if you aren't ready I promise I'll drag you out. And you'll see I can keep my promises better than you can.'

His voice teased, but before she could think of a suitable reply he rang off, and she felt herself crying once more. Brad would never allow her to go, and he was too busy just now to take her anywhere himself. It would be a waste of time asking him. Between now and tomorrow night, she must think of an excuse which would satisfy Rodney and his family without involving Brad. It was all she could do.

On the following day she only saw Brad once, when he sent for her to have coffee with him. Julie would rather he hadn't, as in the typing pool it really started the remarks rolling. The mysterious wound on Brad's forehead had apparently not been so unremarked on as she had thought, and a lot of veiled hints were flying as she left to go to his office. While no one had any proof, it was clear there had been a lot of speculation.

Brad scarcely glanced at her as she drank the coffee which threatened to choke her. He was busy, and, apart from asking if her shopping trip had been successful, had little to say. She began to get the impression that, now he had a sure hold over her, he had lost interest. Or, if he had any left, it was only in one thing. His respect for her had obviously gone.

Suddenly he looked up from the sheaf of papers in front of him, thoughtfully catching the bitterness in her face. 'You realise I have a lot to do before I can get away at the end of the week?'

'You said the same thing about three weeks ago,' she replied sullenly, without thinking.

For a moment she could have sworn he was disconcerted, until he spoke sharply. Ignoring her comment, he said, 'I don't expect to be through here until late, so I won't be seeing you this evening. I imagine you'll have plenty to do, in order to get away yourself. There'll be your packing.'

'Don't remind me.' She tried to copy his grim tones exactly, with an added dash of defiance. Flippantly her lips twisted while unhappiness tore at her heart. Aware of a startling longing to be held close to him, she kept her heavy lashes lowered, knowing she was no match against his astuteness. Didn't he care for her one bit? If only, she yearned, he had.

Quickly she rose, so he shouldn't read the hurt in her eyes, making for the door. 'You were very generous yesterday, Brad, and I shouldn't be spending your time as well as your money. It's a good job I can take a hint.'

'Julie! Stop being so damned stupid!'

Stupid! Incredulously she swung around, staring at him. His face was grim and she seemed to catch a glimpse of strain about his mouth, but who was he to be complaining? Wasn't he doing things his way? He wasn't the one who was suffering! While a few thousand pounds could be of no real value to a man as wealthy as Brad Hewson, it stood for the complete ruin of her life!

'I'm sorry, Brad,' she apologised stiffly, as his glinting eyes stirred a lick of fear.

'You'd better be,' was all he replied, before returning his attention to his work, leaving her to find her own way out.

Julie was late in getting from work that afternoon, but she wasn't worried about it as Joe was away on his trip with Edith so she didn't have a meal to prepare. It was after six-thirty when she let herself in, then did something she had never done before. Going to the sideboard, she poured herself half a glass of whisky. She didn't like the taste of it, but it did make her feel less like breaking down. It mightn't be wise to spend the next few nights in tears, and false courage was probably better than nothing.

Trying to take a firm grip of her emotions, Julie sat down. All of a sudden she decided she would go to Rodney's party. There could be no harm in it, and she had promised to help, as she did every year. She needn't tell Brad. If he did happen to find out what did it matter? His opinion of her could be no worse than it was already.

Just over an hour later she was on her way to the Old Hall with Rodney, wearing a fine blue denim skirt and waistcoat over a snappy checked shirt. It made her look young, about seventeen, and she doubted if it was the kind of outfit to appeal to Brad.

Instead of making her apprehensive, this only filled her with satisfaction. This evening, somehow, it seemed imperative to defy Brad in some way. To do something which might constitute one last act of defiance against a man who was virtually blackmailing her into doing something he knew she considered wrong. If it hadn't been for Joe she would have told Brad what he could do with his money.

She didn't stop to think that a man other than Brad might have demanded even more. Her whole body seemed to throb with despair because Brad didn't love her, and from this a young, feverish resentment seemed to grow and grow.

Rodney, with an alarming disregard for safety, held her hand tightly as he drove. 'Oh, Julie,' he groaned, his fair face sullen, 'I love you. I didn't realise how much until Brad Hewson almost jetted me off to London, but I'm hanged if I'll let that bastard have you!'

'Shush, Rodney!' In spite of her just having finished thinking of Brad in similar terms herself, it had been to herself, and strangely she found herself resenting hearing Rodney criticise him. 'He is your boss, Rodney, don't forget, and you do have a very good job.'

'Which isn't everything! I've known that since I had to leave you. I've decided to get another job so I can stay here, near you.'

They were nearing the Old Hall. Nervously she glanced at him as he released her numbed fingers. 'I don't think you should do anything rash, Rodney. I—I tell you what, let's get some of the work over first, then we can have a chat about it. I—there's something you should know.'

As they circulated, Julie followed by an ill-humoured Rodney, she wondered desperately how she was going to explain anything at all. Why had she been so impulsive? She would have been wiser to have stayed away from here tonight. Surely Rodney didn't love her? She didn't want any man loving her, she thought unhappily, forgetting how only a short while ago she had wished Brad had.

Rodney's mother came and kissed her, handing her some books of raffle tickets, begging her to see if she couldn't get rid of them. 'Lovely to see you, dear,' she smiled.

Julie managed to sell all the tickets very quickly then Rodney and she just wandered around. There was a bonfire and fireworks, then supper. Afterwards, when the children had gone home, there was dancing, both outside and in the ballroom. Everything went past in a blur, although she tried to concentrate. The usual crowds were here. Some came at the very beginning and stayed until the end, while others arrived later, as though content to leave the noisier events of the evening to the younger set.

Julie was drinking too much, which might not have mattered if she had been used to it. Rodney, in as uncertain a mood as herself, frequently replenished her glass without her being really aware of it. She didn't bother to ask where he was getting it from, but what they were drinking was rather different, she fancied, from the relatively innocent fruit cup which his mother was passing around.

Rodney refused to leave her side, she had never known him so determined, but as there were plenty of people about she felt there was no need to panic. She tried once to explain about Brad, but couldn't find the right words, and in the end she gave up. Floating in a champagne-coloured world, Brad didn't seem nearly so important any more. It wasn't until she caught a glimpse of Viola Gardner that she sobered up. Brad wasn't with her, but she might easily tell him that Julie had been there, having fun with cousin Rodney.

With a murmur of excuse to Rodney, Julie dived upstairs, intending only to find a quiet spot where she could sit for a few minutes to clear her head before ringing for a taxi to take her back to the cottage.

CHAPTER SIX

OCCASIONALLY, when she was a child, Julie had stayed at
the Old Hall. The bedroom she had usually been given
was at the top of the stairs. Making for it now, she found
with relief that it was empty, showing no signs of occupa-
tion. Without bothering to close the door she sank down
gratefully on the side of the bed. Putting her head in her
hands, she tried desperately to pull herself together.

A noise startled her. To her dismay, on looking up
quickly, she found Rodney coming towards her.

'Julie!' he was saying sharply. 'What's the matter?'

'Nothing much,' she faltered, wishing unhappily that he
had stayed away. 'If you'd just leave me for five minutes,
Rodney, I'll be all right.'

'How can I leave you like this?' he objected, sitting down
beside her and staring at her tearful face. 'Come on, tell
old Rodney.'

'Oh, don't be silly!' She tried to make light of it. 'It's
nothing, I tell you. I think I've probably drunk too much
of whatever it was you seemed bent on pouring down me.'

'Oh, come on!' he laughed. 'It was just champagne. One
Martini, perhaps, and a little of this and that, but nothing
to make you feel so very terrible.'

'Honestly, Rodney,' she shook her head impatiently, trying to clear it, 'you should have had more sense! You know
I'm not used to it.'

He laughed again and put a friendly arm across her
hunched shoulders, pulling her closer. 'Who wants to be
sensible on a night like this?' he murmured, lips on her
ear.

Suddenly, before Julie knew what was happening, he
was pushing her back on the bed and beginning to kiss her

wildly. She could feel him stretching against her, his muscles tightening, his arms strong as he pinned her down.

Surprise held her immobile for seconds. Seconds during which, with Rodney's lips fiercely on hers, she felt nothing but revulsion. There was none of the wild sensation she knew when Brad kissed her, no urgent response of the senses, and she found herself hating having another man touch her.

'No, Rodney!' she cried, wrenching her mouth away as she struggled.

She must have left it too late, for he wasn't letting her go. 'Julie!' he gasped hoarsely, his face flushed with passion. 'For God's sake have pity on me. Don't you know how much I want you? We've got this far—we can't stop now.'

'No, you're mad!' He was holding her so she couldn't move, his hands pulling roughly at her blouse, sending buttons flying. 'Stop it!' she sobbed.

But he was kissing her again, and suddenly a startling thought shot through her head. Wouldn't this be the perfect revenge? Brad wasn't paying all that money for a girl who had belonged to other men. He knew as well as she did that she had never had an affair. If she gave in to Rodney tonight, wouldn't she be able to laugh in Brad Hewson's face! When they reached Paris.

Tempted beyond everything by a mental glimpse of Brad's reactions when he discovered what she had done, Julie forced her reluctant arms around Rodney's neck. As if relieved by the ease of her surrender, Rodney tightened his grip and he was all over her, kissing her hotly.

Then, just as irrationally as she had made up her mind, Julie became aware she couldn't go through with it. Brad meant too much. She had no idea where the realisation came from, she only knew she loved him. It was suddenly as simple as that. Somehow she must get away from here—she must!

As the situation began filling her with horror, she went

cold, Rodney, raising his head drunkenly, gave her a puzzled look, at the very moment that the door burst open and Brad crashed through it.

Fright worse than anything she had ever known gripped Julie by the throat, as Brad's eyes went swiftly over the couple on the bed. She couldn't breathe, or move, and Rodney seemed similarly afflicted. What was Brad doing here? Never could she remember, as she stared into his face, seeing a man so enraged—so grim. His eyes were glittering with an unholy black fury.

The brief pause at his entry was just that. It was merely seconds before he went into action. One moment Rodney was beside her, the next he was sprawled at the other end of the room. Then she, too, was off the bed, Brad's light denim jacket around her shaking shoulders, after he had taken in the gaping front of her shirt.

'Make yourself decent!' he rasped, his glance going coldly and slowly over her before he turned to a cringing Rodney.

'Didn't you realise,' he asked harshly, 'that Julie and I are engaged? That it happens to be my fiancée you were molesting?'

Rodney's face went almost as white as Julie's, as he slumped back against the wall. 'Your—fiancée!' He looked absolutely shattered. 'I had no idea!' His voice rose weakly, as he turned a bewildered gaze towards Julie. 'Why didn't you tell me, Julie, instead of letting me believe ... I only wanted you because I love you—wanted to marry you myself, and you seemed willing ...'

'She may be willing,' Brad cut in savagely, 'but she happens to belong to me. And you can take it from me that she knows it. I'm not standing here making up fairy tales!'

Beneath his vicious tones Julie found herself swaying, recognising the harsh challenge. Either she played along or to hell with Joe and any protection they might expect from Brad Hewson! But she wasn't his fiancée! Her blue eyes widening, she gazed at him helplessly. What was he playing at? Just what was his game?

Rodney's voice wavered, a croak of protesting resentment. 'Julie, you could have said?'

'But she didn't.' Brad still looked consumed by anger. 'She led you on like a proper little tramp!'

'I ...' Julie stiffened, then paused, aghast to find she didn't really have a thing to say—at least, nothing which might serve as an adequate excuse. She had come to the Greens' party from a desire to escape her own company, not to cheat Brad. It hadn't been until Rodney found her here that bitterness had filled her with a foolish longing for revenge. To explain why she hadn't been able to go through with it was impossible. Even without loving Brad, she knew now it would have been impossible. Yet to give Brad even a hint as to how she felt about him would simply be putting yet another weapon in his hands.

'Yes——' gripping her arms, ignoring Rodney, Brad shook her roughly, 'what were you about to say?'

'Nothing.' Unhappily she stared back at him, deriving no comfort from the iron hard cast of his features. Drawing a deep breath, which she knew Brad heard, she spoke to Rodney. 'I'm sorry, Rodney. This should never have happened. I told you—I mean I think I told you, I'd had too much champagne ...'

Rodney mumbled, 'I wouldn't have given you so much, but I thought you needed cheering up.' Though speaking to Julie, it was at Brad he looked. It was clear that he was beginning to wonder why a newly engaged girl should want cheering up at all.

Speaking grimly, his eyes narrowed into slits, Brad said, 'I suggest you both shut up. I take it you haven't changed your mind about me, Julie?'

Numbly she shook her head, not wanting to think what Rodney must be making of this. She had known Brad was cruel, but she hadn't been aware he was also dangerous. It came to her belatedly that to defy him further might be distinctly unpleasant, both for herself and Rodney.

'Good.' She shrank from Brad's cold satisfaction, as he continued. 'I'd appreciate it if you kept quiet about our engagement, Green. There'll be an announcement in the press, but not until the day after tomorrow.'

'Yes, of course, sir.' Rodney was suddenly very young and sullen.

Brad looked him slowly up and down again, his eyes glinting. 'Julie and I will go now. You understand she won't be seeing you again?'

'I understand, sir.'

Downstairs they went, she and Brad together. Rodney stayed where he was. Julie's arm felt numb as she was propelled along by a force which contained a definite element of violence. Yet only Brad's gripping fingers gave any hint that he was disturbed. To the casual onlooker he might simply have been a man in a hurry to escape with a pretty girl.

Mrs Green caught them on their way out. 'Ah, Julie, just the girl I'm looking for. I need your help in the bar. Rodney seems to have disappeared and I can't think of anyone else.'

'I'm sorry, Mrs Green,' Brad didn't give Julie a chance to reply, 'Julie is coming with me.'

Mrs Green smiled. 'I actually believe, Mr Hewson, that Viola is looking for you.'

'Tell her I might be in touch,' Brad's voice was cool. 'Now, if you'll excuse us.'

'Oh, no ...' Mrs Green's vaguely helpless voice trailed after them, causing Julie to cringe even more than she had been doing.

As Brad thrust her into his car, she rubbed her arm with a hand that trembled. 'You've hurt me,' she whispered as he got in beside her.

'Not half as much as I should have done—as I'm going to,' he snarled. 'I'd bloody well like to kill you! I'll certainly see that young Green leaves the works in the morning.'

'You can't!' Overcome with reaction and horror, Julie felt the tears pouring down her cheeks. 'It—it wasn't Rodney's fault.' She saw Brad's hands tighten on the steering wheel as they turned on a scream of tires. 'It would be most unfair,' she stammered unwisely, 'to sack him.'

'Unfair? By heavens, I wonder you dare suggest it, after what's happened!' Hedgerows whipped past in the most alarming manner. 'You're a proper little bitch, aren't you? How far did you go?' Lividly, as if unable to contain himself any longer, Brad threw the car on to the side of the road, laying hold of her almost before it ground to a halt. Her teeth shook and her head lolled like a waxwork doll's before he released her. 'Well?' he requested savagely. 'Are you going to tell me?'

'I—I don't have to.' She didn't know where that bit of courage came from. Her throat had constricted so that she couldn't speak properly.

'You little tramp!' he repeated, his eyes no blush as the darkness outside, his lips curled back ferociously. 'You made me a promise. I bought you, and what do you do? Get into bed with another man, as quick as you can when my back's turned!'

Through sobs of hurt, she cried, wildly, 'You said yourself that chastity was old-fashioned.'

'You little fool! What do you think I was paying for?'

'I—I didn't know,' she gulped, fearing she did.

'Liar!' he snapped, beginning to shake her again as fresh fury overtook him. Then he seemed to get a grip on himself and suddenly let her go. 'No one would believe I could be such a fool!'

'If you are,' Julie sobbed, 'it's your own fault. I never asked you to ask me to marry you! You didn't have to tell Rodney I'm your fiancée. Anyway,' she hiccuped miserably, 'I know you have no intention of marrying me. I suppose this is part of your revenge—to make me look foolish.'

Sneering at her openly, he exclaimed, 'How else could I have got you out of that bedroom? Would you have liked me to have said : 'That's the girl I'm going to live with?'

'It's common knowledge that you never give an explanation unless it suits you,' she cried.

'In this case I considered it necessary,' he rejoined cuttingly, 'for Rodney Green's benefit, as well as your own. And we are going to be married, make no mistake about that, either, so you'd better start pulling yourself together. I don't want any tear-stained fiancée!'

'No, Brad!' Protesting, she found herself beginning to shiver at the malevolent glitter in his eyes. 'No!' she cried, only to find his arms hauling her to him. 'Brad! You're taking things to ridiculous lengths.'

His mouth sought hers, crushing it, his teeth catching the softness of her skin, making her jerk painfully. Then, just as suddenly as he had grabbed her, he let her go. 'I have to call at Haydon for something,' he said curtly, 'before I take you home.'

Julie was still trembling from the cruelty of his assault when he drew up in front of his house. She didn't think she could have moved, if she had wanted to, when he asked her to wait. She even felt a vague gratitude that he didn't demand she go in with him.

'Don't try running away,' he advised savagely, as though aware this might occur to her. 'It would only be a waste of time.'

Moments later he was back again and, without further words, turned in the direction of the village. As they completed the journey, Julie wondered what it was he had had to call for so urgently at Haydon. Wouldn't it have been easier to have dropped her off first and then gone home?

At the cottage, he added to her uncertainty by asking if he could come in. Sensing that he had no intention of doing otherwise didn't stop her from trying to object.

'I'm tired, Brad.'

'No, you aren't,' although his anger appeared to have abated a little, he still spoke harshly, 'but you soon might be.'

While she wondered about this, he took her key and opened the door. Then he guided her firmly to the sitting room.

Some unconscious sense of self-preservation made Julie ask with forced nonchalance, 'Did you want to see Joe?'

'No,' he said in dangerously silky tones. 'Anyway, how could I? If you're trying to give the impression that he's upstairs, you'd better think again. I happen to know as well as you do that he's not here tonight.'

'I see.' Julie shivered sharply at his apparent ability to read her thoughts. To distract her attention from his tall, powerful figure she stumbled across the room to draw the curtains, then switched on the electric fire. Immediately she wished she hadn't, as this gave a suggestion of intimacy she wasn't seeking.

As he stood staring at her, his eyes hard, she trembled and looked away from him. Never would she be able to understand how she had come to fall in love with him. Already, after she had been aware of it for barely half an hour, it was tearing her apart. How could anything but heartache come from it, this wild, unreasoning longing which was invading every inch of her? It wasn't something she had ever expected to happen, yet, knowing how she felt when Brad touched her, she must have been a fool not to have guessed before now. Love, she was discovering, wasn't a comfortable emotion to live with when it had to be kept secret. Brad would never care for her. He might want her, but that was all.

In frozen silence she watched as he took a small box from his trouser pocket. Surprisingly, for the moment, it wasn't this which held her immediate attention. It made her remember she was still wearing his jacket and without it he must be cold. Struggling out of it, she forgot it covered her torn blouse. Flushing warmly, she dropped the denim jacket on the floor while hastily attempting to do up her two remaining buttons, though they were half hanging off.

'Stop worrying about things that don't matter.' He picked up his jacket, slinging it carelessly over a chair as she tried with dignity to tidy herself up. His glance slid from her hot face to the box in his hand and with a swift flick of one finger the top came up to reveal a glittering ring. 'This was why I found it necessary to call at Haydon,' he explained curtly. 'Come here, Julie.'

Because she felt too weary to protest, she automatically did as she was told. Then suddenly, as she realised what he intended doing, she shrank back, her eyes fixed on the ring which he had taken from the box, with something very like horror in her dilated pupils.

'Brad,' she gasped, the flush deepening on her creamy skin, 'surely there's no need to go as far as this!'

'As what?' he snapped arrogantly, following up her hasty retreat and picking up her left hand. As a quick tremor rushed through her, he thrust the ring without tenderness on her engagement finger. 'If we're to be engaged it has to be official.'

The ring seemed to burn Julie's finger, which was strange when she felt so frozen. She knew little about such jewellery, but it didn't take an expert to see that the ring she was wearing must be worth a great deal of money. The diamonds and rubies glittered up at her, proclaiming a value she didn't want to think about. 'Where did you get it?' she whispered. 'It—it looks terribly expensive.'

His mouth twisted on what might have been a slightly mocking smile. 'You'd find it—terribly expensive to buy. Even the insurance would be beyond you.' He paused, as if studying her startled eyes. 'You can think of it as a family heirloom if you like.'

Numbly Julie stared down at it again, unable to believe it was all happening. The ring was heavy on her slender hand, making her long fingers seem fragile and very white as the stones gleamed against pale skin. Brad, she noticed dazedly, was surveying both the ring and her with grim satisfaction.

'Don't you like it?' he asked.

Silently she nodded, while wondering how she was standing the strain. If only she didn't love him so! She asked wildly, in order to escape her thoughts, 'Why do you want to marry me, Brad? That is, if you really intend to?'

Again he smiled mirthlessly and again his eyes went over her closely, noting the strain in her face, the tautness of her slender young body. 'Circumstances might have trapped me into it, Julie, but I'm growing to like the idea. I haven't been married before and I've tried about everything else. Perhaps a young and beautiful wife can be an asset, something a man with the right authority can mould into being exactly what he wants.'

Julie controlled a tremor of anger at such arrogance, curiosity, for once, calming her tight nerves. 'Have you forgotten you only wanted to live with me? A day or two ago you would never have considered me for your wife.'

His eyes flickered, as though she had touched a raw spot, but just as quickly he was harsh again. 'Maybe I want to make sure you suffer. Married to me you won't find it easy to escape, and a husband does have more legal rights than a lover.'

Turning away, she felt suddenly too distraught to look at him. Misery clutched her and her hands felt like ice. All this might not have been too difficult if she hadn't loved him. This could render her helpless to retaliate, whatever he did to her.

'I still think you're making a big mistake,' she said bleakly, 'but it would be better if you left now. I'd like to go straight to bed.'

'Of course you would.' His voice held something she couldn't quite define, and more than a hint of merciless determination. 'We'll go to bed together.'

His eyes glittered, as cold as the diamonds of his ring,

as he watched her face grow white. 'Brad, you can't know what you're saying!'

'You don't really believe that?' he laughed arrogantly, his mouth hardening at her abject despair. 'I never waste words, I assure you.' He put his hands on her arms, tightening his grasp when she stiffened. 'You were quite willing to sleep with young Green, remember. Are you in love with him?'

Brad's tone suggested it wouldn't greatly concern him whether she was or not, but if he hadn't caught her unawares she might have contrived a more devious answer.

'No, I'm not ...' Finding no clue to his reactions in the blankness of his face, she knew she must make some attempt to explain how that scene in the bedroom at the Old Hall had come about. 'I—I've never loved Rodney, not that way.'

'Then why,' Brad cut in softly furious, 'are you objecting to me?' Without allowing her to continue he said contemptuously, 'I think I'll have long ago forgotten most of what Green knows about women. You have nothing to fear, and you do have my ring on your finger.'

'It's not that, Brad. You must listen ...'

'I'm past that stage,' his square jaw jutted grimly. 'And so should you be, my small Venus. Don't you know how desperately I want to make love to you?'

Not waiting for a reply this time, he crushed her closer, his mouth coming down on hers. He kissed her gently, at first, until he met her initial resistance, which seemed to inflame him. Cruelly his mouth hardened and with one hand behind her silky head he forced her lips apart, deepening the pressure until she found herself struggling for breath.

He was punishing her, she realised, for rejecting him after apparently accepting Rodney, and she supposed she couldn't really blame him. But as she spun, halfway between what seemed like heaven and hell, she found herself responding, in spite of the pain he was deliberately inflicting. Against him her body sagged, as if totally unequal to the task of resisting him.

Brad's searching mouth eased a little, as he felt her feverish fingers lacing through his thick dark hair, and he groaned against her shaking lips, 'I want you, Julie. Before this night's over you're going to know how much. This time I'm not taking no for an answer.'

As she tried to speak his hands were sliding under her ragged shirt, seeking the warmth of her bare flesh, conveying their own message of desire. Deep within her came the familiar instantaneous response, spelling out its note of warning, even while the surging force of her emotions threatened to break through every barrier of common sense.

As though he sensed how she was having a struggle to keep her sanity, Brad began caressing her more passionately, his hands and mouth demanding and forceful, until she was pressing closely against him, as if as hungry for a more intimate contact as he was.

Their bodies were melting together and his voice was husky against her bruised and trembling mouth. 'Come with me, Julie.' Without waiting for a reply, he picked her up and strode with her towards the stairs.

His mouth moved over the silkiness of her hair; the words he muttered were muffled and thick as he let her head fall back over his arm, so he could seek the unsteady pulse at the base of her throat. His lips were warm and exciting, but she knew the real danger lay within herself, as her love for him increased the ardour she had known before until it began searing her like flames.

'There'll be no one here to disturb us,' he said softly, as he strode into her bedroom, kicking shut the door as she slid to the floor.

Dazed, Julie formed his name soundlessly against the coloured softness of his shirt, then tried again. 'Brad, you can't do this ...'

His jaw tight, he stared down at her hot face. 'Yes,' he taunted, 'I can.'

'Please, Brad!' Feverishly she tried to overcome the urgent desire to give in to him, to seek only the sensuous force of his lips. The pressure of his arms was sweet agony. Her voice sank into faintness, leaving only her eyes to plead. 'Please ...'

'You let young Green do worse.'

'No, you're mistaken! He didn't touch me ...'

The quality of his passion became merciless. 'You don't mean to tell me that he carried you upstairs, in front of all those people, against your will. You must have walked up together—or were you waiting for him, already in bed?'

Her head bowed as her breath drew guiltily. When it came to it she found she couldn't lie blatantly. What a fool she had been! Why hadn't she realised that this man who was holding her now was the one she wanted—whether married or not? His hands were hot on her skin, his mouth making her wince, as her silence seemed to condemn her immediately.

'I've told you before, Brad, you don't understand,' she gasped, lightheaded as her traitorous body responded unerringly to his anger, rather than being repulsed by it.

'I didn't take a degree in human biology,' he quipped savagely, 'but it took no expert to understand what I saw. You meant to cheat me. Maybe you have, although from the look of your boy-friend I doubt it, but I mean to find out, one way or another.'

'Let me go!' Julie was suddenly hysterical, torn ferociously by the wild strength of her own emotions. Why—why was she pleading with him when her hands were clinging to his hard shoulders, when all she really wanted was to sink beneath the sweeping waves of sensation rushing over her?

'I'll never let you go.'

Julie closed her eyes against the pitiless glitter in his as his mouth returned to hers and her heart leapt in response. She was drowning in his deep, sensual kiss, and he didn't stop until she lay helplessly against him.

'Now,' he said, with oppressive triumph, 'shall we go to bed?'

Knowing she was too weak to deny him anything, she laid her head on his breast, taking deep, painful breaths against his thundering chest, while fear and a strange ecstasy made her limbs tremble.

'Now,' Brad muttered violently, his arms closing around her.

As he swung her up again in his arms to carry her to the single narrow bed, a car pulled up outside, shattering the midnight tranquillity. Julie heard Brad mutter something darkly under his breath before saying in louder tones, 'It looks as though we have company.'

Turning abruptly to leave her, his jaw rigid, he said grimly over his shoulder, 'I'd better go and see who it is. If it's young Green . . .'

It wasn't. It was Joe, looking no more surprised to see Brad than Brad apparently was to see him. As Brad drew him into the sitting room, Julie ran downstairs, so it would seem she had only been in the kitchen. Outside the sitting room, she heard Joe explaining.

'Edith wasn't well—an attack of migraine. It was no use staying away. She tried to settle, but all she wanted was to get home to her own bed.'

'Didn't you want to stay and look after her?' Brad asked tersely.

'She doesn't want me, sir,' Julie could have cringed at Joe's humble politeness, 'says she's better left alone.'

'Good God, man, there must have been something you could do!' Brad sounded so harshly impatient that it came to her instinctively, he would never have left someone he loved to fend for themselves, not if they were ill. He had been prepared to treat Julie callously—but then he had never pretended to love her.

Cold with a prevading misery, she entered the room and Joe began explaining all over again.

Then, with a start, she heard Brad say, 'Well, you're just in time to congratulate me. Julie and I are engaged.'

Julie went to work next day with deep smudges under her eyes, but if she had none of the radiance common to most newly engaged girls, Joe didn't appear to notice. Yet he could only think of Julie's engagement. He didn't even seem to have a thought to spare for poor Edith, not until Julie advised him to ring to see if she had recovered.

After Brad had gone, last night, shortly after he had made his startling announcement, Joe had been frankly elated.

'Tell me,' he had chortled, rubbing his hands together, in a way Julie was beginning to hate, 'how did you manage to bring his lordship up to scratch? A blind man could see he fancied you, but I never thought he would ever marry you!'

White to the lips, Julie had refused to answer, while wondering, not for the first time, however her mother could have married such a man. Sometimes she wondered if there had been a side to her mother that she hadn't known about, as Joe had a certain crudeness about him which she herself couldn't have tolerated in a husband. No matter what came of her engagement to Brad, she knew she wouldn't go on keeping house for Joe much longer.

At breakfast, still happily unaware of Julie's disgust, Joe had exclaimed suddenly, 'I've just thought, Julie dear, I won't have to sell my car. Brad surely wouldn't dream of sueing his prospective father-in-law!'

Coldly, Julie stumbled to her feet. 'I'm not sure yet how Brad will regard you,' she said enigmatically, as she went out.

Before he had left last night, Brad had arranged to have lunch with her. As one o'clock came around she wished he hadn't, she had never felt less like eating in her life. All morning Julie had been tense, waiting for things which had never happened. Rodney didn't attempt to get in touch,

and Joe for once had apparently managed to be discreet, so
no news of her engagement leaked out. It was she who had
asked Joe to say nothing, recalling what Brad had told
Rodney and taking it for granted he wouldn't want Joe to
tell anyone either.

Brad's beautiful diamond ring, which Joe stubbornly
maintained was brand new and must have cost a fortune,
Julie popped in her handbag, wondering if Brad would ask
for it back. She didn't think he would. Confused, she stared
at it before dropping it deep into one of the pockets. Why
did Joe refuse to believe it was a family heirloom? If Brad
did ask for it back, she wasn't sure how she would feel.
While such a thought should have been pleasing, she was
bewildered to find that it wasn't.

As she rinsed her hands before going to meet him, it
struck her despairingly that last night had been another
occasion when Brad and she might have become lovers.
Maybe she ought to be feeling grateful towards poor Joe,
instead of criticising him. Once again her pulse raced as
she dwelt apprehensively on what might have happened if
Joe hadn't turned up. It was no use deluding herself that
Brad would have let her go this time and, remembering
the urgency of her own response, she shivered. How much
longer could she hope to escape from the vengeance of a
man who had no love for her to soften his desire for re-
prisal? But how much lasting satisfaction would there be
in shared passion, without love? This would be all they
had. Brad had given her a ring, but she didn't believe he
would ever stoop to marrying her.

He had asked her to meet him outside and she found him
waiting at their usual place. As she climbed in the car
beside him, he glanced immediately from her pale face to
her bare hands, and his mouth went thin.

'The cause of such pale cheeks is obviously our engagement,' he said dryly, 'but all other evidence of it
appears to be missing.'

'You—you mean my ring?' Huddling in her corner, Julie flinched at his sarcasm. As he nodded, grimly, she explained, 'It's in my bag.'

'And where has it been all morning, might I ask?'

'Why—in the cloakroom.'

'My God!' he was softly vehement. 'Where anyone could have taken it! A ring worth—— Oh, never mind ... But she tells me she left it lying in the cloakroom!'

'Listen, Brad,' suddenly she was facing him, bright flags of colour in her cheeks, 'if it's as valuable as all that, why give it to me? Something from any cheap store would have served the same purpose.'

'Be quiet!' His voice grated with fury and his eyes sparked. 'Do you think any future bride of mine would wear a cheap ring? If I'm annoyed it's because you've obviously never been taught how to value anything.'

'That's not true!'

He paused, watching her clenched hands, the two single tears which ran down to her trembling mouth, the furtive, childish movement of her tongue as she licked them off.

'Julie,' he said harshly, 'I'm much older than you. You must allow me to know what's best, in some things, anyway.'

Numbly she nodded, averting her damp face, not finding sufficient immediate control to argue. Brad's expression was cold and still, he obviously had no sympathy for her wild outburst.

With steel in his tones he said, 'I want you to take my ring from its hiding place, Julie, and put it back on your finger. Suppose you wear nothing else, I want to see that.'

His eyes were very steady, as he looked at her, steady and implacable, painting mind pictures which slightly altered her breathing. Again she nodded, swallowing a lump in her throat as she obeyed him, hearing his suppressed sigh when she took a few minutes to locate it. On finding it, she was so unnerved that she pushed it clumsily on her finger, as though it was indeed a bauble of little value.

Brad's mouth tightened, but he took her hand, studying it with the same satisfaction he had shown the evening before. 'You must remember,' he said silkily, 'never to take this off again. I want everyone to know you belong to me.'

Julie was silent as he edged the powerful car in and out of the midday traffic, wishing she could take comfort from his words. He spoke like a man determined to get what he wanted, without having to explain his reasons. These she might never know.

Restlessly she stirred beside him, taking her eyes from the grey-clad elegance of his legs to stare blindly at the city streets. Much between them had gone wrong, since the evening he had asked her to live with him, and it was obvious Brad blamed her and his tolerance was finely edged. He had about him the air of a man who wouldn't stand much more, and Julie wasn't sure what to make of him. It was becoming clear he had his anger and contempt on ice until he had her wholly at his mercy. Brad Hewson, she realised hollowly, wasn't a man to forgive past slights, even if he was diabolically clever at hiding it!

CHAPTER SEVEN

THEY lunched at a smart restaurant near the centre of the city. Conscious of her plain skirt, Julie wished she had worn something different, but the outfits she had got for Paris wouldn't have been very suitable for a morning at the office. Not without causing unwanted comments. What did it matter? she thought disconsolately. She didn't know anyone here, and if some of the other diners bestowed on Brad an occasional pointed glance, he didn't take any notice.

Paris! Julie's memory jerked painfully and she glanced at Brad quickly. Because of its frightening implications she dared scarcely think of it. Did he still intend taking her there? Not having stopped to consider her somewhat changed position, she wondered now if it would make any difference regarding Brad's basic attitude. An engagement was easily broken, especially one like theirs which didn't really mean a thing.

As the meal progressed and Brad made no fresh disclosure about Paris or anywhere else, she began to worry desperately about what was to happen next. He didn't talk much after seeing she was comfortable and settling what they were to eat, but concentrated instead on jotting figures down on a pad, which Julie presumed had to do with his afternoon's work. His neglect, she concluded unhappily, must be meant to demonstrate what he really thought of her.

At last, unable to bear it any longer, she pushed her plate away practically untouched and asked wearily, 'Do I still leave at the end of the week?'

His eyes went flinty, as if he guessed all the fearful uncertainty contained in that one query. 'Yes, Julie, you still leave at the end of the week,' he echoed mockingly, 'but there has been some change of plans.'

In the small pause which followed, during which she suspected she was meant to sweat a little, Julie found herself studying his face, with a kind of odd fascination. It was strange how often she felt she was seeing Brad Hewson for the very first time. Always she seemed to find something different in the firm hardness of his features. Today she noticed how fine his dark grey eyes were under the forceful brows, and how deeply cleft was his chin beneath the sensuous lower lip. But again it was the ruthlessness in his demeanour which disturbed her most.

'Are you listening, Julie?'

His impatient tones brought Julie swiftly back to reality. Anxiously she nodded, as he allowed her to deviate no longer. Because he looked so arrogant, fear struck her afresh, but she managed to whisper, 'You said there'd been a change of plan?'

'Yes. I intend taking you to Sussex to meet my grandmother, who is about the only relative I have left. Once I promised, perhaps rashly, that if ever I should decide to marry she would be one of the first to know. I thought we might spend a few days there, then come back here while I complete a few urgent matters of business and see about a licence. We should be married within the next two or three weeks, no longer. It might have been sooner, but I intend having a lengthy honeymoon, which will include our postponed trip to Paris.'

Julie's eyes widened as she met his cool, level stare and she digested this startling information. He couldn't be serious! Wasn't it just clearly ridiculous, two people, sitting opposite each other, regarding each other like strangers and talking of marriage? For Brad to take her to see his grandmother was surely carrying this deception too far. It was one thing to deceive Joe, but she drew the line when it came to sweet old ladies. Besides, some of those old ladies were not easy to deceive. Brad's grandmother might soon guess he didn't love his fiancée. And what then?

'Brad,' Julie protested bravely, 'you don't really want to marry me. Why not call the whole thing off?'

'No.' His eyes gleamed darkly, in sudden anger that she continued to defy him. Leaning towards her his voice was coldly emphatic. 'Haven't I told you, Julie, I've never wanted any woman so much, and I mean to have you, one way or another. You didn't like—or you pretended you didn't like—the first way I suggested, and as you more or less trapped me into the second you must be prepared to make the best of it. We'll begin by doing things properly, as you seem set on such a course, and if that includes a visit which doesn't appeal to you, then you must look on it as part of the price you must pay for your much vaunted respectability. Taking everything into account, I don't think you have anything to grumble about, my dear, so can we please consider the matter closed?'

He might have been in the boardroom! Even his mention of wanting her had such an unemotional ring to it that she doubted, in that instant, if it had anything to do with love, or even desire. Maybe, as he had once hinted, his need of a wife was because of other things, which might include a son and heir? All the same, she wished she didn't have to go and meet his grandmother. This sparked off a quick flicker of apprehension, but she dared not mention it, not with Brad sitting regarding her with such a formidable expression on his face.

'Brad,' she protested rashly, 'I—I don't recall actually stressing respectability, but the—the other way didn't seem right, somehow.'

'Not for you, as you are now, perhaps, but you would soon have stopped complaining.' His mouth twisted at her hotly flushed face. 'You don't have to pretend. You wanted the smug triumph of a wedding ring, and this is what you're going to get. So stop whining!'

The way he spoke made her flinch, and she clenched her fingers tightly, feeling almost as angry as he looked. He sounded as though he hadn't the least bit of feeling for her, and hurt made her exclaim defiantly, 'I still think we'd be silly to marry so soon, feeling as we seem to do about each other.'

Brad rose, flicking his hand for the waiter as he stared down at Julie. Coldly he said, 'As you've no choice in the matter, I'd advise you to forget it. You're simply wasting both my time and your own.'

They went to Sussex that weekend. Julie, who had never been to Sussex before, knew she would have looked forward to such a visit in any other circumstances. The countryside was new to her and with another companion she might have asked numerous questions, but she found Brad's silence daunting. He made no attempt to talk to her, and she wondered unhappily if he was beginning as he meant to go on. What was the future to be like if he was to treat her like this, outside the bedroom? Somehow she doubted if such a relationship could survive long. Powerful cars, priceless rings on her fingers, huge houses to live in might be the answer to many a maiden's prayer, she thought cynically, but it certainly wasn't hers.

Depression weighed heavily as she glanced at Brad's taut profile. There was no tenderness there, no concern that she shouldn't be too anxious over her forthcoming meeting with his elderly relative. Brad wanted to marry her only to prevent her from running away each time his back was turned. At first he had considered he had been more or less tricked into an engagement, but the idea had obviously taken hold in his mind as being the most effective way of gaining what he wanted.

Yet each time Julie thought of their marriage she didn't know how she was going to go through with it. If only she hadn't been trapped by Joe's criminal foolishness she might have found some way of escaping Brad, but as things were this was virtually impossible. Not without bringing down recrimination and shame on Joe's head.

There were few other motorists on the road, which lay

hushed and quiet, shrouded in November fog. Julie hoped they would get there before the weather turned worse and Brad's grandmother grew anxious.

Since Brad told her they were coming here, she had thought a lot about his grandmother, apprehensively curious as to whether this would be the same woman who, with her husband, had taken Brad's father off to the South Coast to prevent him marrying her mother. Julie's heart thudded with a mixture of hope and fear. Brad hadn't said his grandmother had lived at Haydon Hill, but even if she had it didn't follow that she would connect Julie Gray with her mother. She would have known Julie's mother by another name.

If this woman was the one Julie feared she would be, and the story did happen to come out, what would Brad say? He was proud, but surely he wouldn't hold that against her, especially when it had all happened so long ago. Perhaps she should tell him herself, before they got there. Glancing at Brad again, for no good reason she could think of, Julie decided not to.

They stopped for lunch. It was well past one before he swung off the main road to the front of a rambling old hotel.

'We'll get something to eat here,' he smiled tauntingly, taking her by surprise. 'I hope you're hungry, Julie darling?'

Darling! Before she could prevent it, Julie drew her breath in sharply.

'My grandmother will expect it,' he rejoined sardonically. 'She's very astute.'

'It must be a family failing,' Julie snapped, hating his dry tones. 'I suppose you were merely practising for her sake?'

'Yes.'

A lance went straight through Julie's unsteady heart and it hurt. Stubbornly she forced herself to speak of something else, to ignore Brad's narrowed gaze. 'What if your grandmother doesn't like me, Brad?'

He smiled tightly, as he leant over to unfasten the seat belt she had forgotten about. 'It's quite possible she won't, but only because she doesn't like strangers. She's getting too old.'

Something drove Julie to say bleakly, 'We don't really know much about each other, do we?'

He hooked up her belt, looking slightly bored. 'About our respective families, you mean? Is it necessary?'

'It's usual . . .'

He turned his head, so his face was near and every nerve in her body seemed to quiver. 'But our relationship isn't usual, Julie. I know you'll agree?'

Feeling his eyes on her so closely, she lapsed into silence. As close as this he interrupted her thought pattern, so her mind grew too confused for logical arguement. 'If you say so,' she murmured at last, knowing she must do something to break the sudden tenseness between them.

Grimly he sighed as he straightened away from her. 'I thought I'd already told you I don't have any relatives apart from this one grandmother, and as our life together won't have anything to do with hers, whether she likes you or not is irrelevant.'

Throughout lunch Julie found it impossible to forget what Brad said. Wasn't he making it clearer, each time he mentioned it, that theirs wasn't to be a normal marriage? Mutiny stirred in Julie's heart as she realised she was going to be kept very much out of sight. Even if he had dozens of relatives, Julie Gray wasn't to be introduced into the family circle, in a manner which might have suggested any permanency. Again she suspected Brad would find some way of getting rid of her as soon as he tired of her. As for her mother—it wasn't as if she had done anything wrong. In fact, Julie knew, it was her mother who had been wronged, and one day, if Brad tried her too far, she might tell him so. She might also tell him that in overlooking Joe's crime he was probably only making long-overdue retribution!

'We'll stretch our legs for ten minutes,' Brad said lazily after they finished eating. 'I could do with some fresh air after being in the office all week, and it will be dark before we reach Arundel. Tomorrow, if the weather clears up, I might show you something of the town and the South Downs, but tonight that won't be possible. I'm afraid you'll have to content yourself with looking at me, and my grandmother, who you're determined isn't going to like you.'

Julie, trying coolly to ignore his taunting tones, went with him along a narrow country road, but she wasn't sure that she wanted to. The thick white fog persisted, giving the overhanging branches of trees a weird, ghostly look. Drops of water fell from the skeleton branches above their heads and the mist pressing in on them from all sides seemed to deaden every sound, even their footsteps. It brought an odd sense of isolation. Julie felt as though she and Brad were the only two people left in the world, lost on a lonely planet, floating on seas of grey cotton wool space.

'Let's go back, Brad,' she whispered, somehow fearing to speak loudly in such oppressive silence. Brad had obviously forgotten all about her. He was striding along, his face down, the thick dark hair ruffled on his deep forehead which creased as though he was deep in thought. 'Brad!' this time she raised her voice deliberately, in order to attract his attention, 'I'm going back to the car. I don't care what you're going to do.'

He halted so suddenly she almost walked into him. His head came up and she saw the wide, square chin, jutting and pugnacious. She shivered, but put it down to the cold and damp as his hand came out to catch her as she fleetingly lost balance. 'Right,' he agreed grimly, much to her astonishment. 'It isn't the best of days for walking.'

Something in his eyes mystified her for a second, causing her to speak impulsively. 'For a man with everything, you sound more like one with nothing!'

His glance flickered warily before his mouth quirked with lazy coolness. 'Why should you think I'm feeling depressed?'

'I—I don't know,' she floundered, wishing she hadn't suggested it.

'And,' he went on incxorably, holding her widening eyes, 'you appear to hold the view that a man with money has no right to feel depressed. Don't ever,' he said cynically, 'make the mistake of measuring happiness in terms of hard cash.'

'It's easy enough to talk,' she mocked, trying to sound careless while her nerves tightened at his hardening face.

He continued to look hard at her, his eyes darkening with a smouldering anger. 'Sometimes, Julie, you sound and look so young, I wonder if I haven't taken leave of my senses.'

'Just because I mentioned your money ...'

His eyes compelled her to hold their stare and he looked as if he could have spanked her. 'To make money, Julie, I work like the devil, and I'm not always sure if it's worth it. Still,' his mouth curled jeeringly, 'a man needs this commodity to afford the good things in life—a girl like you, for instance, though unfortunately you're rarely—good!'

She would have liked to have hit him then. Colour tinted her skin, but she managed to regard him steadily and retort distinctly, 'I hate you, Brad Hewson. I really do!' With fury raging tumultuously inside her, she didn't find it difficult to believe it, not then.

'You've made that quite clear,' he rejoined with deadly softness, making no attempt to touch her with anything else but his lancing gaze. He took pleasure, she saw, from the way she quailed, and she wished, not for the first time, she was better at hiding her feelings. His eyes glittered like black ice and she wondered if he had any idea how hard and domineering he looked when pride reminded him of his position in life, that he was boss of a huge company employing thousands of people. Men like Brad Hewson must often imagine they wanted to be ordinary, but they wouldn't know where to begin.

'All you want to do is to hurt me,' she whispered uneasily, against his prolonged stare.

Curtly he brushed aside her trembling protest. 'Hating me the way you do, Julie, I can't see how I can hurt you, although I'm certainly going to enjoy trying. And, before you start hurling insults, you might remember how, over the past few weeks, you've had little consideration for me, even when your stepfather robbed me. One more thing might just prove the last straw.'

Brad's grandmother was one of the most regal-looking women Julie had ever seen, and she might have admired her greatly if she had been a little more friendly. As Brad and Julie were late in arriving, she was already dressed for dinner. She sat in the drawing room talking to a tall, dark girl, who ran to meet Brad as soon as she realised he was there.

'Brad darling!' Taking no notice of Julie, the girl flung her arms around his neck as she reached him. Julie felt a dismayed flutter in her breast as she saw him being warmly kissed. 'Oh, Brad,' the girl cried, 'I've been so looking forward to your coming. I've missed you, darling.'

'You always have,' he smiled, catching the girl's face lightly between his hands and kissing her back. 'How are you, Ruby?' he asked.

Julie tried not to watch as misery tightened her throat, and she wished fiercely that Brad would put this girl Ruby away from him. She wasn't such a fool as to imagine his life had been one of celibacy. At his age he wouldn't have been normal if he hadn't sought some feminine companionship before now, but surely he didn't expect to entertain both his fiancée and an old girl-friend under the same roof?

Perhaps this girl hadn't been his girl-friend, but she seemed to be making it fairly obvious that, at some time or another, they had shared an intimate relationship. She was laughing up at Brad, shamelessly patting his cheek while he continued to smile back at her.

Swallowing hard again, Julie turned away. What was Brad playing at? If he was trying to make her jealous he wasn't succeeding, but of course, he wouldn't be doing that. It wouldn't even occur to him.

As Julie moved it appeared she was noticed for the first time. The girl's eyes suddenly narrowed on Julie's slender figure, then widened insolently.

'I didn't notice you weren't alone, Brad. Don't tell me you're having a working weekend and brought your secretary with you?'

'No, Ruby.' Gently he unlaced her arms before turning to Julie. Mockingly his eyes found hers, making his intentions clear, and when she tried to evade him, one of his hands locked around her waist like steel as he drew her forward.

Thrusting her nearer the elderly lady, sitting a little way from them, he said suavely, 'Grandmother, I once promised that you would be the first to meet my fiancée.'

While Ruby caught up and stood beside them looking stunned and making no effort to disguise it, his grandmother was made of sterner stuff. 'Who is she?' she asked, staring at Julie, as though she believed her ears deceived her.

'My fiancée.' Brad didn't seem to mind repeating it, but regarded his grandmother steadily and Ruby not at all. 'Miss Julie Gray. I'm sure you'll be glad to hear my bachelor days are almost over.'

Mrs Hewson drew herself up sharply, bristling with disapproval. 'You could have let me know, Brad. I'm much too old to have surprises like this sprung on me!'

'No, you're not,' he replied calmly. Then, 'Aren't you going to say hello to Julie?'

If it hadn't been for Brad's arm around her, Julie felt she might have sunk through the floor. She wanted to, the atmosphere was terrible. Only Brad appeared to be enjoy-

ing it. She knew, from what he had told her, that his grandmother was in her late seventies, but she looked at least
ten years younger, with the physical and mental energy of
many a woman half her age.

After a few tense moments, Mrs Hewson actually smiled
and held out her hand, but Julie felt far from reassured.
It didn't really matter, she tried to tell herself, whether Mrs
Hewson liked her or not, and instinctively Julie felt she
didn't. As she took the wrinkled old hand in her own, she
was tempted to blurt out, 'Don't be too upset, Mrs Hewson.
Your grandson doesn't love me. He's only marrying me
for amusement and—and other things. It will be a marriage,
if it ever comes to that, without permanence.' Only the
presence of the girl Ruby stopped her.

Ruby Carter was the girl's name. Brad introduced them,
a slight smile on his mouth, a watchful glint in his eye
which warned Julie to behave herself. Other girls could
apparently do as they liked, but she couldn't! Julie's own
lips were too stiff to manage more than an unnatural grim-
mace, but she hoped he noticed she did try.

Ruby said sharply, her face going red, not pale like
Julie's, 'Isn't this rather sudden, Brad? You never mentioned anything when you rang me last week.'

He replied, expressionlessly, 'Not really. And it was
you who rang me, if you remember.'

Ruby withdrew, but with a mutinous expression that
clearly hinted that she wasn't yet defeated. If Mrs Hewson
wanted rid of Julie, and was looking for an ally, she would
certainly find one in Ruby Carter.

After a little more general conversation, Julie was relieved
when Brad rang for the housekeeper to show her to her
room. Apart from that one smile, Mrs Hewson hadn't
thawed much, and Julie was glad to escape.

Later, when she came down again for dinner, she felt
almost happy to learn that Ruby had gone and she would
only have Mrs Hewson to face. Mrs Hewson mightn't be
prepared to like her, but at least she didn't present the same

threat as Ruby did. And, without Ruby's demanding presence, Brad might decide to spare a little time to be nice to her.

Ruby not being there, however, was to make no difference. This Julie soon discovered. In the drawing room, she found Mrs Hewson exactly where she had left her and waiting, with a marked lack of patience, for her dinner. Julie was aware of relief when the door opened and Brad appeared. Mrs Hewson, for all her grumblings, didn't seem to share her feelings and Julie suspected she had been spared the ordeal of a barrage of questions by his timely intervention. Perhaps she ought to have waited for him upstairs, as she had felt inclined to do. It had only been the fear that he might attempt to make love to her that had brought her rushing down in such a hurry.

Julie wore a blue silky dress which brought out the deep, dazzling blue of her eyes. She wore no jewellery, apart from her engagement ring, and was startled when Brad, under the pretence of claiming a fiancé's right to kiss his loved one's cheek, murmured coldly, 'Where are your earrings?'

His lips stung her soft skin and the flame which flashed through her caused her breast to heave, in a manner which drew his attention. Trying to edge away from his tall figure in the immaculate dark suit, she hissed defiantly back, 'Upstairs.'

'Tomorrow night you will wear them, just as you will remember not to shrink every time I come near you,' he advised silkily, before escorting his grandmother to the dining room.

After this Brad almost ignored her, talking mostly to the older woman, without apparently worrying as to what conclusions his grandmother might draw from his blatant neglect of his fiancée. At first Julie felt shaken and cold, but eventually managed to compose her emotions to give some semblance of indifference. Dully she watched the light from the overhead chandelier playing on Brad's face, as he and Mrs Hewson talked of local people and places of which Julie knew nothing.

Someone who was referred to as an interfering old busybody had told Mrs Hewson that the house must be getting too much for her, and she spent the whole of the first course convincing Brad, and presumably herself, that it was not. He agreed with her, but as though his mind wandered, that there was no reason why she shouldn't continue living here, if she was content.

Nodding with satisfaction, Mrs Hewson raced on about other things, but, as though following Brad's lead, she also almost ignored Julie. Yet all along, Julie knew intuitively, Mrs Hewson was very much aware of the slender slip of a girl, sitting so quietly at the table. The strange little nobody who had the audacity to imagine she could become her grandson's bride! The atmosphere wasn't exactly enjoyable during the otherwise pleasant meal, but Julie doubted if her two arrogant companions even noticed. It seemed to her that the evening would never end.

The next morning she was startled but not really surprised when the housekeeper asked if she would go to Mrs Hewson's bedroom, after breakfast. It sounded such an imperious summons it would have given Julie a great deal of pleasure to have declined, but she decided sombrely that it mightn't be worth the effort. Mrs Hewson was obviously of much the same mould as Brad. If she had something to say very few people would be able to prevent her. Mrs Hewson would make sure there was another opportunity, if Julie refused to see her now.

When Julie asked where Brad was, the housekeeper informed her politely that he had gone out but hoped to be back for lunch. Pretending to accept this casually did nothing to halt her inner dismay, but her faint nod appeared to satisfy the housekeeper, as she withdrew.

While pouring herself a cup of coffee, which she suddenly didn't want any more, Julie wondered dismally where Brad had gone. He must have been perfectly happy to have gone off, leaving her on her own, assured that, as she knew no one, she couldn't get into any mischief.

Ignoring the covered dishes of cooked food, she began nibbling half-heartedly at a piece of dry toast. It had been too dark when they arrived last night to see much of the house and grounds, but she had the impression they were both large and well kept. Certainly the interior of the house was spacious. Glancing wryly around, Julie wouldn't like to have priced some of the very beautiful antiques. Even more wryly, she decided Mrs Hewson couldn't be short of a penny or two. No wonder Brad didn't want to displease his grandmother! This place must cost a small fortune to run and looked even larger than Haydon Hill. On the other hand it must provide employment for a lot of local people, which could only be a good thing.

Distraction wasn't the easiest of arts to practise, she acknowledged with a sigh, as her thoughts swung tenaciously back to the one man she didn't want to think about. Had Brad gone to see Ruby Carter? Hadn't he said, as the girl left to go home yesterday, that he would see her tomorrow, which would be today? Ruby's face had lit up when he said that, especially as he hadn't paused to consult his fiancée. The flash of triumph in Ruby's eyes had been unmistakable, as she departed. A tremor passed through Julie, even now, just to think of it.

Wearing a soft cream-coloured shirt with neatly tailored camel pants and a matching, sleeveless jacket, she found her way to Mrs Hewson's room. Anything was better, she supposed, than to sit fretting at the breakfast table all morning.

'Come in,' Mrs Hewson called, in answer to Julie's slightly nervous knock.

Mrs Hewson was in bed, reading the morning paper, the bedrest propped comfortably behind her suggesting that this was her normal routine. Over the top of the newspaper, before laying it down, she glanced at Julie coldly. 'You don't look like a newly engaged girl,' she greeted her bluntly, staring almost rudely at Julie's colourless cheeks. 'I should have thought any girl who'd received a proposal from my grandson would have been feeling elated! How did you manage it?' she asked sharply, when Julie made no reply. 'Ruby Carter didn't, and it wasn't for the want of trying. And I should think she's a lot smarter than you.'

Smarter—as in brains, and probably looks as well? Julie had to concede this, if only to herself. Slowly she closed the door, watching Mrs Hewson despondently. She had become too used to Brad's callous remarks to be surprised by those of his grandmother. Ruby Carter had more than good looks, she was obviously extremely sophisticated and worldly, something which Julie knew she was not. She could find no comfort in what Mrs Hewson had unintentionally betrayed about Ruby trying to capture Brad and failing. Brad clearly thought no less of Ruby because of that!

Murmuring a belated good morning, Julie tried to speak with dignified composure. 'Those are questions that Brad might answer better than me.'

Unimpressed, Mrs Hewson snorted, 'Men get carried away by a pretty face and figure, especially if it's a new one. I just hope Brad isn't making a mistake.'

Feeling curiously driven, Julie challenged, 'Does this mean you don't approve of me?'

'How can I tell, girl, when I don't know the first thing about you?' Mrs Hewson retorted querulously, waving Julie rather belatedly to a nearby chair, as if reluctant, in her case, to remember common courtesy. 'I would like to see Brad settled, but not because I can't wait to see his son and heir. I stopped worrying about things like that long ago. I'm more concerned that you're a girl of his class, or at least respectable. A little education can too easily disguise a girl's true background. You may look refined and beautiful, but your people could be riff-raff!'

Furiously, her cheeks scarlet, Julie jumped to her feet

again. 'Mrs Hewson,' she gasped, 'I don't have to stay here to be insulted!'

'You will only be that,' the old woman replied, haughtily unrepentant, 'if what I say applies to you.'

'I—I wouldn't care to call anyone that!' Julie retorted fiercely, yet she found herself obeying weakly when Mrs Hewson waved her indifferently back to her chair. For all her pulse raced with indignation, she supposed, while she was here, she might as well hear the lot! Bitterly she wondered why Brad had left her at the mercy of his grandmother. He must have a peculiar sense of humour to deliberately expose her to such a merciless attack!

Feeling so deeply wounded that she was forced to blink back tears, she waited despairingly as Mrs Hewson continued, 'You can't really be surprised that I'm concerned for Brad's happiness, Miss Gray. Since his parents died I'm all the family he has left.'

'I'm sure we both know he's more than capable of looking after himself,' Julie couldn't help observing dryly. Without knowing why, her voice changed as she heard herself adding bleakly, 'Anyway, there's always divorce.'

Unfortunately her remark misfired. Mrs Hewson pounced, with scornful decisiveness. 'I don't approve of it, but your mentioning it only emphasises my point. Half the divorces today are through people marrying without having anything in common. This I firmly believe!'

Julie felt ashamed that she was unable to resist asking wistfully, 'Don't you consider Brad and I have anything in—in common, as you put it?'

The old woman's glance became sharper and she shook her head. 'You're wearing Brad's ring and there's something about the way in which he looks at you, but quite frankly I'm not happy. Where do you come from, Miss Gray?'

Cold to her very toes, Julie replied evasively, 'The village near Haydon Hill.' Fervently she hoped Mrs Hewson didn't remember.

It was quite obvious Mrs Hewson did, from the way her eyes narrowed suddenly. 'I see,' she frowned reflectively, pausing for a moment as she focussed closely on Julie's face. 'In small communities, I've found it's not uncommon for people to resemble one another. You have the look of a woman I once knew. Someone who for all I know might still live in Little Wrighton.'

As Mrs Hewson continued to regard her intently, Julie knew it could only be a matter of time before she discovered exactly whom Julie Gray was! In an attempt to divert her, she shrugged awkwardly, 'A lot of people from Derby live in the village now. They commute from the new estates, and I'm afraid I know very few of them.'

'I used to live at Haydon Hill myself, a long time ago,' Mrs Hewson began, with what seemed suspiciously like renewed determination. Julie could almost feel her annoyance when the telephone by the bedside rang, cutting through what she was saying.

Acting impulsively, Julie grasped the opportunity such an interruption provided. With a muttered excuse, she rushed to the door and escaped.

Returning to her room, she found herself wishing feverishly that she hadn't come here. Brad had more or less forced her to, but maybe she had given in too easily. This morning she felt cold and alone, with the events of the past few weeks crushing her spirit. Had Brad, on seeing Ruby Carter again, also realised the futility of such an artificial engagement? Wearily, Julie sighed. Brad must surely have been wrong in asking her to live with him, but she must have muddled her handling of subsequent events badly, to have finished up in the fix she was now in. Now she appeared to have nothing but Brad's contempt. This and the ring which gleamed so mockingly on her finger. Brad had never pretended to approve of her and, only a few minutes ago, Mrs Hewson had made it very plain that she wasn't satisfied with his choice, either!

CHAPTER EIGHT

FOR the next two hours Julie wandered around the extensive grounds, trying to keep her mind occupied, in a vain attempt to shut out all thoughts of Brad spending the morning with an old girl-friend. But, try as she might, such thoughts obtruded. What were they doing? Where had they gone? How could Brad be so cruel as to humiliate her like this? Unhappily she recalled Viola Gardner. Apparently he didn't intend dropping these other women just for the sake of his fiancée. Not that Ruby Carter seemed very happy; perhaps she had suffered at his hands, too. It seemed that any woman who was foolish enough to love Brad Hewson was doomed to get hurt.

At last, almost worn out by her turbulent emotions, Julie retraced her footsteps to the house. It wasn't until she was on the actual doorstep that she noticed how last night's fog had cleared to leave a beautiful morning.

Brad was there for lunch, but there was no sign of Ruby Carter. He was alone. Not having seen him come in, Julie was startled to find him having a drink with his grandmother in the drawing room. Still feeling chilled from her slow process of the gardens, Julie felt colder than ever on meeting his distant glance.

After pouring her a sherry, he carried it to where she had wandered, by the window. After speaking to Mrs Hewson and being granted no more than a unfriendly nod, she had retreated, finding even the November sunshine more warming.

She shivered sharply on turning to find Brad by her side. 'Were you wishing you were miles away, like your thoughts?' His dark gaze didn't flicker a fraction. 'Grandmother tells me that you've been out most of the morn-

131

ing. I thought you would have been keeping her company. She would like to know you better, and we won't be here long.'

Somehow, at that moment, Julie found the censure in his voice hard to bear, especially when she didn't feel she deserved it. Not this time! Involuntarily, she took a step back. 'Was that why you went out with Miss Carter?' she asked unwisely.

Instead of giving her her sherry, he placed it with cold deliberation on the window-ledge. He straightened, then taking hold of her shoulders he stared at her, his eyes glittering. 'So that's what you think I've been doing all morning. Amusing myself with Ruby Carter?'

'You might have been ...'

'Ah, now you're not sure?'

'How was I to know?' Unsuccessfully, Julie tried to wriggle away from him, gasping at his leashed sarcasm. The room was huge, his grandmother some distance from them, but Julie could feel her curious gaze. 'You were pleased enough to see each other last night!' She didn't know how her voice and huge, shadowed eyes held a kind of pained accusation.

'Maybe because we more or less grew up together—but,' he added cynically, 'we didn't share the same pram. Nor, with this particular lady, have I ever shared the same bed, despite what you're so obviously thinking. Actually, you might be interested to know, Ruby's way ahead of me in some things. She has one marriage and a divorce chalked up, while I'm only just beginning.'

'I'm—I'm sure she has designs on you, all the same.'

'Julie,' his mouth thinned, 'do you want to get hurt?' Suddenly, as if they were completely alone, he slid his hands to her face, his thumbs coming forcefully under her softly rounded chin to press her face up. The glitter in his eyes deepened, but he took his time in lowering his head until his mouth touched the surprised parting of her lips. Exercising the merest pressure, he kissed her sensuously,

and while his touch could only have been described as
gentle, she couldn't remember feeling so threatened.

When he raised his head, his eyes were hooded and
dark as he looked at her. 'You mustn't forget,' he warned,
his voice low so only she could hear, 'I've paid quite a
lot for you, which means you must forfeit the right to
criticise anything I choose to do. I was about to tell you
where I've been this morning, but it might be better left
to your vivid imagination.'

That afternoon, which she had expected to pass under
a cloud of disapproval, Brad surprised her by taking her on
the promised tour of Arundel. Resolutely Julie tried to pull
herself together and enjoy the novelty of new surroundings.
To have a holiday away from home at all was a rare treat
for her, although she didn't mention this to Brad. The girls
he admired would be those capable of flitting from one
fashionable continental resort to another, with never a
tremor of uncertainty to disturb the even tenor of their
days.

Julie was unable to decide if Brad enjoyed showing her
around, but he did prove a more than adequate guide, and
once when she expressed surprise that he apparently knew
the area intimately, he reminded her that he had been
brought up here. As they surveyed the battlemented walls,
the massive keep and turrets of Arundel Castle, above
which was flying the flag of the Duke of Norfolk, Earl
Marshal of England, she wondered aloud why Brad had
decided to leave his grandmother's home to live at Derby.

Releasing the brake of the car, he moved on. After pointing out the fourteenth-century church of St Nicholas,
which flanked the castle, and the Roman Catholic cathedral
of St Philip Neri, built by the fifteenth Duke of Norfolk in
1868, he said quietly, 'Perhaps I felt my roots were in
Derby, rather than here. I believe, but for an unfortunate
affair with a woman who was determined to marry my
father, I might never have lived anywhere else.'

The afternoon was bright and warm, but Julie felt suddenly cold. So Brad had been told about that, of something which had happened before he was born. It was too long ago to concern him, but he sounded as though he bore a personal grudge. How would he feel were he to discover she was that same woman's daughter? Clasping her hands tightly, Julie almost confessed, there and then, for there seemed no reason why she should make a secret of it. If Brad hadn't sounded so censorious she might have done, but she hated the way he spoke of her mother. Her mother would never have been guilty of such undignified behaviour as Brad suggested; Julie was sure of that. No, let him wait and find out after they were married. It was only right that he should have his share of shocks.

As they went down the High Street she heard him drawing her attention to the Norfolk Arms, a fine eighteenth-century coaching inn, and asking if she would care for tea. When she shook her head and said it was too early, he wondered if she would like to drive to Littlehampton, on the coast.

'Arundel is always crowded on a Saturday afternoon,' he said. 'Littlehampton is usually much quieter, at this time of year, anyway. We can always get a cup of tea there, as well as a breath of sea air. It might bring some colour to your cheeks and make you look a bit more pleased with life.'

Why must he always spoil things? Julie nodded stiffly, her happier mood evaporating. 'You don't have to put yourself out for me, Brad. Littlehampton sounds nice, but won't your grandmother be expecting us back to have tea with her?'

'She usually rests in the afternoons,' he replied briefly, as they set off down the roadway. As he glanced at Julie, his mouth tightened. 'You must learn to be a little more enthusiastic. I have no wish to marry a girl who can't stop looking like a martyr.'

'Just because I mentioned your grandmother . . .'

Abruptly he cut in, 'You didn't tell me you'd had a

session with her upstairs, this morning. I just learnt of it from Mrs Montgomery as we came out. What did she want to see you about?'

Julie started. At lunchtime she had realised, from his guarded answers of Mrs Hewson's queries, that he had spent most of the morning in the estate office going over her affairs. Julie had blushed guiltily, unable to meet the mockery in his eyes, to learn that her suspicions, which she had voiced so indiscriminately, had been without foundation. Yet the humiliation she had felt had not been unmixed with relief, a feeling which had warmed her until this moment.

'I know my grandmother,' Brad went on when Julie pondered on her answer, 'and while I don't think I owe you any great consideration, I would have spared you one of her "third degrees" had I known.'

Startled into replying, Julie exclaimed, 'Oh, it wasn't as bad as all that!' Sharply she bit her lower lip, not quite certain what to say. 'I think she would like to be sure that I'm not marrying you for the wrong reasons.'

'Such as?' tightly.

'Your money, I suppose.'

'You think I'd allow anyone to marry me for that?'

'Men do get married for their money,' she reminded him dully, 'and I'm sure they won't all be idiots. I didn't like to mention to your grandmother that you're the one who's marrying for the wrong reasons!'

'At least I know what I'm doing!'

'What matters most,' she countered, with bitter despair, 'is that you're enjoying it!'

'I intend to.' He caught her wrist and his grip was cruel. 'I'll enjoy, as much as any man can, marrying a somewhat tarnished angel, but that's between you and me. I don't wish my grandmother to hear of it.'

As they reached Littlehampton, Julie averted her face so he shouldn't see the pain in her eyes. He intended to wound and he managed to, but she wouldn't give him the satisfaction of seeing her flinch. She suspected he knew she was, in some way, deeply attracted to him, and this made her vulnerable. Just as long as he didn't discover the true depth of her feelings she might be able to cling to her last vestige of pride. If he hadn't been so much older and experienced it might have been easier. She could only try, but she wished he wasn't so adept at unearthing the very things she wanted to hide.

Littlehampton was a small, ancient port at the mouth of the Arun. Now it was a popular holiday resort and yachting centre. For a while they wandered about the harbour, but it was too cold on the sea-front to linger long. Julie agreed eagerly this time when Brad suggested tea, and followed him without argument to the nearest hotel.

During the next hour he seemed to have little to say to her, and she decided with a heavy heart that it must be a long time since he had found any pleasure in her company. Why couldn't he have been more like Rodney? There was no hidden depth in Rodney to torment a girl. Rodney had always been happy-go-lucky and fun-loving, but Brad Hewson was much harder to read. Yet Rodney's caresses had left her unmoved, while Brad's stirred a breathless rapture that melted her body, each time he kissed her.

As Julie drank her tea she watched him closely from under the thick frame of her lashes. Since she had come to his grandmother's house, her feelings for him had grown confused. She was seeing a side to him she hadn't seen before, or hadn't noticed before. Here, in an environment far removed from their evening outings and the factory, she was aware of some change in him. Perhaps it was the way he went about his grandmother's business, his cool air of quiet authority which she hadn't previously recognised or understood. By comparison she began to feel too naïve, too young, too lacking in everything, apart from the bare essentials, in everything he would need in a wife.

On top of this she sensed a new hardness in him. As she dwelt on it with some apprehension, she realised it had been there since he had discovered her in that bedroom with Rodney. Since that evening when she had thought he was going to kill her, his regard for her had obviously changed. Whereas before, even when he was asking her to live with him, there had always been a kind of respect, now there seemed nothing but contempt. Now his regard was cold and calculating, his whole attitude towards her deliberately cynical. Daily he demonstrated that his wasn't a forgiving nature, and like a cat with a mouse he was merely biding his time.

That evening she decided to wear the other dress she had brought with her, one of the few she had purchased for Paris. She hadn't been too happy about bringing it, but had felt desperately in need of something which might give her some confidence. Unfortunately the dress, which in the shop had appeared to make her look coolly sophisticated, produced now an entirely different effect. It made her seem very young and virginal, as the creamy material brought out the alabaster quality of her skin and gave to her beautiful eyes and mouth an expression of extreme innocence.

'Oh, no!' she whispered aloud, finding something in her reflection she didn't understand but which she knew instinctively would arouse Brad's scorn.

It seemed cruelly appropriate that, at that moment, her bedroom door should open and Brad stroll in. In her bedroom she had begun to feel safe, certain he wouldn't obtrude in so intimate a place, not in his grandmother's house. Startled to find she had been mistaken, she stared at him, not knowing which vexed her most—his arrogant conceit that he was welcome, or the way in which her heart had started to beat.

'You don't mind me coming in like this, do you?' he asked silkily, his eyes going over her but without expression.

'Would it make any difference if I did?' she accused, more occupied in trying to steady her racing pulses than in the diplomacy of her answer. At any time he had the ability to alter her breathing, but seeing him dressed for the evening she found it impossible to resist his dark attraction. She hoped he would just taunt her a little and leave. Surely he couldn't attempt more—in the circumstances?

'None,' he replied, closing the door and glancing around. 'You're comfortable here?'

'Would you care if I wasn't?' she shrugged, challenging him without meaning to.

Having half expected him to ignore her rather trite query, she felt chilled by his reply. 'Not for you, personally, but officially you are my fiancée and, as such, I won't have you slighted.'

'Yet you do it all the time!'

'That's a privilege you granted me yourself, by your own behaviour.' The sudden harshness of his voice was frightening, as was the smouldering blackness of his eyes.

Belatedly Julie wished she had held her tongue, or choosen her words better. Numbly she closed her own eyes tightly for a second, in order to keep back tears of remorse. Impulsively she whispered, half turning from him, 'Did you really believe what you thought you saw that evening?'

'Julie!' he exclaimed tersely, his mouth a ugly line of hardness, 'I didn't come here to go into that.' Swiftly he flicked back an immaculate cuff. 'It's almost seven-thirty and you know how my grandmother hates being kept waiting.'

'I didn't intend keeping her waiting,' she returned, trying to speak mildly as she stooped to pick her small evening bag off the dressing-table.

'Wait a minute.' From his pocket he drew a necklace,

a perfect thing of beautifully glittering stones. As she gazed at it in surprise, he said calmly, 'I promised you this as it matches the earrings I gave you, which I'm glad to see you're wearing tonight.'

Drawing a sharp breath, Julie looked at him. 'Perhaps I'm finding it less painful to obey you, in some things.' Uncertainly her eyes flickered to the jewelled circlet in his hands. Tonight she wore his earrings, but the necklace was something else again. If it had been offered with love, instead of just from a desire to improve her appearance, she might have accepted it with pleasure.

Tautly she went on, her tone defiant, 'Do you really believe I can't remember what you said? You said I should have it if I pleased you. It seems to me that I've never done that.'

'Why is it you can always remember things of no importance?' he snapped coldly. 'Circumstances change. You can have this now—and attempt to please me later.'

Colour racing to her cheeks, Julie held out her hand. 'You always hold the trump card, don't you?'

'That's the secret of success, my dear.' He ignored her hand. 'If you want to make an issue of it, that's what we'll do, but if you'll just stand still I'll put this on for you, and it will all be over much sooner.'

While knowing the feel of his fingers on her bare skin was going to be an ordeal, she did as he commanded. She had the sense to realise it was no request he had thrown at her! Relief washed through her when he accomplished the task quite easily and quickly, scarcely touching her at all.

'There,' he murmured, with grim satisfaction, pointing to her mirrored reflection. 'Don't you think that looks very fitting for a Hewson bride?'

To hide the hurt in her heart, Julie exclaimed sarcastically, 'You don't really imagine you can disguise all my shortcomings with a few pretty trinkets?'

For the second time in her life she thought he was going to murder her. A dull flush came under his skin and his eyes glittered more than the stones around her slender neck. With a quiver of fear she saw his knuckles go white as his hands descended tightly on her shoulders. Then, just as it seemed he was about to snatch her roughly in his arms, he flung her away from him. 'Come,' grabbing hold of her again, as she stumbled against the bed, he forced her in front of him out of the room. 'I believe I heard the dinner gong. We'll go down now, before you completely spoil my appetite.'

This evening, as on the previous one, there were only the three of them at dinner, and it proved a no more comfortable meal than lunch had been. Julie, feeling miserable, could only summon the ghost of a smile as she tried to answer Mrs Hewson's questions. She was very conscious of Brad's dark, enigmatic gaze dwelling watchfully on her, and found it almost as hard to endure as his grandmother's calculating one, as the old woman tried to assess the value of the gems which sparkled against Julie's throat and fingers. It wasn't difficult to see she knew exactly where they had come from.

Afterwards, Julie was surprised to find herself almost relieved when Ruby Carter and some friends arrived. Nothing, she decided, could be worse than having to sit for the remainder of the evening under Brad's chilling regard, fencing with his grandmother's sharp curiosity. Yet the lightening of Brad's expression cut her like a knife when Ruby sailed blithely in.

Mrs Hewson insisted that the new arrivals join them for coffee, and for a while the conversation was general. Then one of the girls asked Julie and Brad when the wedding was to be, and both Mrs Hewson and Ruby seemed to lapse to a stunned silence when Brad replied, 'Within the next fortnight.'

'So soon?' Ruby managed eventually, with a coy glance, a forerunner to the sharper one she directed at Julie's momentarily distressed face.

'As soon as possible,' he smiled grimly, throwing what

Julie supposed was meant to be a loving arm around her suddenly trembling shoulders.

As no one seemed inclined to probe for further details of the wedding, someone suggested they play cards and there followed what to Julie was a rather uninteresting game of gin rummy. During an interval, while Brad rose to fetch drinks, Ruby, obviously quite at home, switched on the TV.

'Just to see what's on,' she cried gaily, while hissing at Julie, under the cover of background music and Brad's absence, 'You'll never get Brad to the altar. He belongs to me!'

It was almost twelve when Ruby and her friends departed, and Brad asked if she would like a last drink. Still shaken from Ruby's sly attack, Julie felt she could have done with one, but she found herself shaking her head.

Mrs Hewson, who had played cards with undiminished energy from the beginning, bade them a tart goodnight, but as Julie made to follow, Brad held her back. 'I won't be long,' he said. 'We can go up together.'

After making sure the huge front door was secure, he escorted her upstairs. 'What was Ruby whispering about?' he asked casually. 'You looked rather startled, I thought.'

Julie laughed as they paused outside her room, but it was completely without mirth. 'She was just warning me off.'

'And you find that funny?'

Julie sobered, her face becoming shadowed and white. 'Not really ... But considering everything ...'

'I always do.' His dark brows drew together slowly. 'You're trying to say that because you don't care for me Ruby's crazy remarks hurt no more than pinpricks?'

About to deny this fiercely, Julie caught herself up in time. 'Is that an accusation?' she murmured instead.

'I think so. Yes. I think it's about time you learnt something of yourself.' Brad was smiling too, but his smile held no more humour than her own had done. 'As soon as we leave here, I think you have a lesson or two to learn, some which are long overdue.'

Grimly, without wishing her goodnight, he left her, but something in his voice kept her staring after him long after he disappeared through a door, further down the corridor.

Shivering, she turned sharply at last, determined not to spend the whole of the night trying to solve his devious remarks. He could only have been trying to hurt her, as he did all the time. It would be something else in the morning! Tomorrow, though, was their last day, and she wouldn't be sorry. If Brad did intend they should marry within the next two weeks she was sure his grandmother wouldn't be pleased. Sadly she tried not to think of that, either. Little good it would do her, longing for approval where it simply didn't exist.

She had been fiddling with the necklace absently for several minutes before she realised she couldn't release the catch. Knowing she could never sleep with the weight of it around her neck, she tried again and again, until a light perspiration beaded her brow. Hopelessly she sighed, collapsing weakly on the nearest chair. There was nothing for it but to go and ask Brad. She dared not disturb Mrs Hewson.

It occurred to Julie that if she hadn't watched him go into his bedroom she might never have known where it was. Ready to feel grateful for even this much, she hurried down the corridor, gathering her defences as she went. He would realise it wasn't her fault. He must have known the catch was difficult. She would much rather have asked anyone but him, but there just wasn't anyone else!

Outside his door she waited, feeling nervous at his surprise when he came in answer to her knocking. 'It's your necklace, Brad,' she felt her cheeks grow hot and added quickly, 'I can't get it off.'

His mouth quirked jeeringly at her obvious apprehension. 'Why, come in, Julie—I feel honoured. It's good to know that I'm the first person you thought of.'

The softly spoken taunt stilled her as she was about to step inside. She said wearily, her face showing visible signs of strain, 'You must know I wouldn't have bothered you if I could have found someone else. And you can easily undo the catch here.'

'The light isn't good enough,' he stepped back politely, opening the door wider, 'and I'm not accusing you of anything. I should have guessed the catch would be difficult.'

Lulled, that he was ready to admit the fault was his, Julie walked past him with a brief nod.

'Here, let me see.'

Her eyes flickered round the large bedroom, not unlike her own, then obligingly she bent her head, putting her hands up to part her hair as she did so, so that it wouldn't get in his way.

'If you'd told me about it,' she said unsteadily as he brushed aside a few strands she had missed, 'I could have asked you downstairs. You must have known.'

'But I didn't know, my dear Julie.' Carefully he did what was necessary before easing the necklace from around her neck, taking care to avoid catching her delicate skin. 'I admit I should have thought of it, but I don't think I've even looked at it since my mother died.'

'Oh.' Forgetting they were alone in a quiet room and it might have been wiser to have gone straight back to her own, Julie turned towards him. 'Does that mean you've never offered it to another girl?'

'A man doesn't offer this kind of thing indiscriminately.' A bleak smile flitted across his face as he stood regarding her. 'I don't happen to have had a fiancée before. Until now I've kept my wits about me.'

'I see,' she said slowly, not sure whether the emotion which flipped through her was happiness or despair. He looked perfectly serious, but one could never tell with Brad Hewson. 'Thank you for getting it off, anyway. And

you'd better put it somewhere safe. The earrings, too.' Too
hastily she began pulling them off and a small cry of pain
escaped her before she could prevent it.

'Julie!' Impatiently he caught her wrist, stilling her
agitated movements. 'I've never known such a fuss made
over a few pieces of jewellery!' Expertly, it seemed to
Julie, he removed those too. 'You'll have to see about having
your ears pierced,' he said curtly.

'I don't like the idea,' she replied, nursing her tender
lobe as she stared at the glittering gems which he weighed
absently in his hand-before throwing them down on the
bed. Belatedly she began edging nearer the door, as she
suddenly remembered where she was and that while she
was fully dressed, Brad wore only a short dressing gown.
Imagining a few sharp words might banish the startling
hunger in her heart, she exclaimed, 'I won't have it done,
either, no matter how many times you suggest it!'

As if his sense of humour was as strained as hers, he
turned on her harshly. 'You seem determined to object to
anything I suggest! When I first knew you, you weren't
nearly so hard to please, and for a little while after Joe
defected you were willing to agree to almost anything. Well,
let me warn you, my dear, that if you think my ring on
your finger is a kind of licence to do as you like, you're
mistaken. Nothing has changed. I'm marrying you because
it seems the only way I can get what I want, but don't expect any rewards for withholding all you have to give until
after the wedding.'

Julie turned so cold she felt numb and tears stung her
eyes, and she lowered her lashes as his eyes bored mercilessly into them. 'You know as well as I do that a lot has
changed since we first met. It's not just me ...'

Taking no notice of her strangled little protest, he asked
grimly, 'Didn't you enjoy yourself tonight?'

Confused and anxious, she raised her head again to
look at him. 'I'm not sure,' she faltered. 'I suppose so, in
a way ...'

'In future,' ruthlessly he brushed aside her uncertain words, 'whether you're enjoying yourself or not, you will look as if you are. I find myself getting extremely tired of your self-pitying expression!'

If he had struck her, Julie knew she couldn't have felt worse. He sounded as though he hated her, and she saw his face through a haze of pain. The tears she had been holding back flooded her eyes, running down her cheeks, almost choking her.

'Oh—don't! Oh, God ...' Brad muttered, frowning. 'Why do women always weep?'

'I'm—I'm sorry ...' She had no handkerchief and had to wipe her streaming face with her hands, and as his eyes rested on her she trembled.

'Here, for Pete's sake!' he ground out harshly. 'It can't be as bad as all that!'

As she blindly shook her head his arms came out to draw her protectively against his shoulder. Taking a handkerchief from his pocket, he attempted somewhat clumsily to mop up her tears. 'Come on,' he said, pressing his hard cheek against her hair and rocking her a little, as if she was an infant he was cradling in his arms. He had, apparently, a normal masculine discomfort of a woman's tears but was doing his best to hide it.

'Julie, hush!' Her continuing sobs seemed to affect him strangely, as he stroked her head awkwardly but gently. 'Be quiet, Julie. You'll make yourself ill!'

His shoulder was broad and like a haven to the distressed girl. For a few moments she wanted nothing more than to be held closely. She clung to him shuddering. Where before there had been only coldness, now there was warmth, and she could feel the love inside her responding to the gentleness of his touch. It was so long ago that he had held her like this, she had forgotten how sweet it could be.

'All right?'

'Yes.' On a trembling sigh she tried to draw away from him, as his practical tones brought a swift return of the tension which wouldn't allow her to relax. 'I don't think this will improve the self-pitying expression you spoke of.'

He didn't let her go, but stayed silent, his hand still stroking her glossy hair. Julie was ashamed at how easily she allowed him to hold her close again, as a great weakness invaded her spirit. To be here with him like this seemed a kind of benediction.

At last she stirred as the new peace she had found was disturbed by other, more insistent emotions. A tremor passed through her and she had to control a dangerous impulse to put her arms around his neck. His charm for her was magnetic, but to give in to it would only spell more misery. If she had to give in, she must wait until she was sure there was no other way.

'Julie?' His voice startled her swimming senses to a drugged obedience. As she lifted her head their eyes locked and held and in his there was a momentary flare of something she couldn't define. 'Julie, I didn't mean to hurt you. This weekend ...' he hesitated. 'Perhaps it was a mistake to bring you here. It doesn't seem to have solved anything.'

'Did you really expect it to?' she asked softly, not wanting to destroy the feeling of affinity between them, yet terribly afraid she so easily might.

'I had hoped——' Again he paused, his voice strangely roughened. Laying his hand firmly along her jaw, he examined her tear-stained face. When she closed her eyes a muscle jerked at the side of his mouth. 'Sometimes Julie, I begin to wonder what I've done to you.'

'How do you mean?'

'I'm not sure. Nor am I quite sure what you're doing to me. Right at this moment all I want is to make love to you, and frustration isn't easy to live with.'

Her mouth parted, but her small flutter of denial came too late. His head bent and his mouth was on hers, refusing to allow any evasion. Hard hands held her shoulders as, against her will, her body curved to his sweetly and everything else ceased to exist.

How long they remained like that she was unable to judge. Brad wrapped his arms all the way round her and her heart lurched as she felt his lips caress her cheek. He kissed the tip of her nose, then trailed to tease the lobe of her ear, and when he claimed her mouth again she was lost. Her lips parted beneath the insistent pressure, and, as though he sensed a change in her, he began to caress her more passionately, his mouth becoming demanding and forceful.

Julie, recognising the change herself, didn't understand it but wasn't frightened. Floating high on a wave of sensuous emotion, she shivered but didn't flinch as he slipped the slender strap of her dress from her shoulder and his hand found the warm fullness of her breast. While her stomach turned over crazily she didn't shrink away.

When he lifted his head her lips felt bruised and trembled slightly. The strength of his arms hurt, too, yet she realised her own arms were tightly round his neck, her fingers fiercely entwined in his thick dark hair.

He was staring down at her, his eyes very alert and sensually alive, but as a tremor passed right through her and she made a distressed sound he gently disentangled himself.

'Julie——' he began, when the door opened and his grandmother walked in. She had knocked but hadn't waited for an answer, possibly thinking Brad would be in bed. Julie, though startled and embarrassed, felt no sympathy for the older woman's expression of shocked amazement as she found the two of them together.

Brad drew back, but slowly, not obviously disturbed by his grandmother's precipitous entry. If there was a glint of anger it was instantly quelled. 'Do come in,' he said silkily, as Mrs Hewson hesitated. 'After all, it's only midnight.'

He spoke without any apparent deference to Mrs Hewson's age and Julie saw the old lady draw herself up with dignity. 'I didn't expect you to have company, Brad, or I shouldn't have intruded.'

Hoping it might help, Julie said unsteadily, 'If you'll both excuse me ...'

'Not yet.' Brad's hand tightened on her arm, which he hadn't yet let go of. Deliberately he smiled, in a way which made Julie's cheeks grow hot. 'You and I still have—unfinished business, my dear, while I'm sure Grandmother won't be staying long.'

'I most certainly shan't!' With a forcefulness which surprised Julie, the old woman exclaimed, 'You may appreciate my untimely intervention more, Brad, when I tell you about a telephone call I've just received from a friend. Someone in Derby, who couldn't ring me earlier as she's been out to dinner.'

Brad raised his eyebrows dryly. 'Don't tell me the city's on fire?' he drawled.

Unimpressed, Mrs Hewson gazed at him coldly. 'The news I have concerns your fiancée,' she snapped. Her eyes, now sparkling maliciously, swung to Julie. 'Years ago we were forced to come here so that your father might escape the undesirable attentions of a woman who could never have made him a suitable wife. Did you know that this girl whom you've been foolish enough to become engaged to happens to be that same woman's daughter?'

CHAPTER NINE

JULIE could feel the colour leaving her face as she stared at Mrs Hewson in despair. She felt rather like a hunted animal, having the same terrible feeling of being cornered. Not until this moment did she fully realise how much she had wanted to protect her mother from any possible repercussions because of her own involvement with Brad. She might have known that all her efforts would be in vain.

Brad didn't speak immediately, but the grip of his hand on her arm threatened to crush her bones. 'Is this true?' he asked, taking no notice of his grandmother's start, as his question appeared to throw doubt on the veracity of her accusations.

To Julie the coldness of his tones proclaimed his disapproval, even before he voiced it. It was quite clear he was ready to condemn her mother out of hand, without waiting, or wanting, to hear the true story.

'I believe so,' she replied hopelessly, avoiding looking at him, not because she felt guilty but because, especially after being held so closely in his arms, she couldn't bear to see his open contempt.

'Why didn't you tell me?'

Surprised at his even tones, she raised her head, finding his eyes closely on her but with nothing in them to give any hint of how he felt. Encouraged a little, that he wasn't obviously furious, she faltered, 'I didn't think it was relevant and—and you must know why.' Lifting her chin slightly, she looked defiantly at Mrs Hewson. 'It happened a long time ago, and I'm not convinced my mother was guilty of the things you speak of.'

Again Mrs Hewson drew herself up as though affronted. Ignoring Julie completely, she said coldly to Brad, 'I'll leave

149

you to draw your own conclusions, Brad. You know the facts, and if you continue with this foolish engagement I wash my hands of you.'

'Why didn't you mention this yourself?' As the door closed tartly behind his grandmother, Brad turned to the agonised girl by his side, his voice cold as steel, now he had her alone. 'It would surely have been less dramatic than what's just taken place?'

'No,' she choked, fighting vainly to free herself as his hands moved harshly to her shoulders, 'Oh, I don't know! I could have told you. Don't think I didn't think about it, but I was frightened you would send me away.'

His voice came dryly. 'Isn't that what you would like?'

'But then you would punish Joe ...'

'Ah ...!' Understanding brought the silkiness she had come to fear back to his tones. 'I see! I can still do that, you know.'

'Yes, I do know.' Her voice cracked as sudden weariness caught it, yet pride forbade her to plead. 'You'd better go ahead, there's nothing more I can do. Because of my mother your grandmother will never welcome me.'

'And you believe I would allow that to influence me?'

His breath on her cheek was agony. So that he wouldn't guess, she said sharply, 'Mrs Hewson must have seen some resemblance, something which reminded her of my mother when she looked at me, and because she was clearly thinking of her at the time. I was always told that in looks I take after my father's side of the family, but perhaps it was some slight expression. Whatever it was, I consider your grandmother has acted with your future happiness in mind, and surely you must have some respect for her opinion?'

'In certain matters,' he agreed, 'but not personal ones.'

'But this—this concerned your father!'

'Exactly,' he sounded bored. 'And while I understand your mother was no better than she should be, it still makes no difference to you and me.'

Julie took a deep, angry breath. 'I wouldn't marry you if that's the opinion you have of my mother! I refuse to believe what you say of her. I have my pride, too.'

Brad's hands tightened, then fell abruptly from her shoulders which, without his immediate support, began trembling. 'You forfeited your right to that a long time ago,' he said flatly. 'First your mother, then your step-father, to say nothing of the cheating you did yourself with Rodney Green. Now you would like to cheat me again, but I'm afraid I'm not as indulgent as the other men in your life appear to have been. This time I'm going to see you honour your commitments.'

The next morning was like some frightening anticlimax to something she had dreamt. At eight Julie crept downstairs in the dawn-darkness of a November morning to discover Brad breakfasting alone.

'Good morning, Julie,' he rose as she entered. 'I've just finished, but help yourself.'

He spoke as if nothing had happened. As though he hadn't dismissed her, a few hours ago, from his bedroom with anger and contempt in his voice. Now there was nothing, his face was quite expressionless; she might have been a casual acquaintance in whom he had no particular interest.

Julie couldn't pretend so easily. Even ordinary politeness was getting beyond her where Brad was concerned. Nervously she pushed up the sleeves of her thin blue sweater, as she sat down, then pulled them hastily back over her wrists again as she realised what she was doing.

As Brad's eyes followed her jerky movements, his mouth tightened, but he made no comment. Unable to stand the peculiar silence, Julie stared dully at the white tablecloth, her fingers clutching at the cup of coffee he had poured for her. Coffee, to which he had added sugar and milk without asking if she wanted either.

'Are we not leaving this morning?' Julie couldn't

imagine, after that awful confrontation with his grand-mother, how they could stay. Brad might, but she must certainly get away.

He shrugged, his only concession of sympathy. 'No, Julie, we can't leave yet. I'm afraid I still have things to see to here. I was actually just on my way out.'

Julie sighed, trying to affect a calmness she didn't feel. 'Your grandmother won't want to see me around.'

'Maybe not,' indifferently he pushed back his chair, 'but if I'm to straighten out her affairs she must be prepared to put up with a little inconvenience. She's had her own way too long and it's turned her into a stubborn old woman. However,' his eyes assessed the paleness of Julie's face, the anxious uncertainty she was doing her best to hide, 'we should be on our way shortly after lunch. In the meantime, I suggest you eat a good breakfast, then take a walk round the grounds. The air will do you good, and, as far as my grandmother is concerned, I don't think you need see her again before we leave. On Sundays, if I remember cor-rectly, she always lunches with a friend after church.'

In spite of her hopes that Brad might finish his business early, it was after four before they got away. Julie, con-trolling her apprehension, had made a point of seeing Mrs Hewson and thanking her for her weekend, but the old lady had brushed aside her thanks abruptly.

'No good will come of it, my girl,' had been her parting salvo, as she had swept out regally to where her chauffeur waited patiently.

With troubled eyes, Julie had stared after her. If Brad had loved her it might have mattered to him that his grand-mother didn't approve of her. For him, Julie had tried to forget the insulting way in which Mrs Hewson had spoken of her mother, and tried to be friendly, but it had been a sheer waste of time. Feeling sad and humiliated, her anger gone, Julie had turned and gone to her room to pack her few belongings. Even doing this had made her feel she was trespassing, and she had been glad to carry her suitcase down and wait for Brad in the hall.

Silently she sat beside Brad now, as they travelled once more through the unfamiliar countryside. It grew dark and she shivered, as the grey skies darkened in tune with her thoughts. Brad drove fast, although with his usual care, and the powerful car ate up the miles. At this rate it wouldn't be long before they were home.

At last he commented, 'I hope you aren't brooding over my grandmother, or your mother? What happened regarding your mother doesn't matter any more. The past isn't important. If I was startled, it was because you hadn't told me.'

Julie sat stiffly, but didn't try to be evasive. 'I did wish your grandmother could have liked me.' She paused, reluctant to discuss her mother, for all Brad's unexpected tolerance. Hesitantly, she said, 'Your grandmother must miss you dreadfully.'

'Not really.' He dipped his headlights for an approaching vehicle. 'Two strong characters rarely get on, not at close quarters. I wasn't much older than you when I went to live in London. I don't believe she was sorry. I keep in touch, of course.'

'Didn't you find London lonely?'

'No. I had various schemes, even then, for expanding the business.' His broad shoulders lifted with slight deprecation. 'I expect I was too young and brash, but I'd just left university and was extremely ambitious. Of course in those days I hadn't the expertise, but I soon acquired it.'

Without moving, Julie fell silent again. He had done that, all right. According to the gossip, he had gone through the entire company like a brush through a dusty room and never looked back since. Ruthless efficiency, coupled with that touch of genius, for which many English executives were still renowned. Brad Hewson had a clever brain and knew how to use it, but he was calculating, too hard. This was how she had once heard him described. Glancing at him sideways, taking in his taut strength, his controlled vitality, Julie shivered.

'Cold?' he asked, seemingly attuned to her slightest movement.

'No,' she glanced away from him, hoping he couldn't so easily read her thoughts, 'I—I think I must be tired. I was out most of the morning in the fresh air.'

'How did you sleep last night? Or didn't you sleep at all, after you went to bed?'

His tone, so clearly hinting that this was the true cause of her weariness, made Julie flush. Unsteadily she exclaimed, 'Must you refer to that?'

'Not particularly, no.' His voice cooled. 'But I refuse to drop every topic of conversation which doesn't appeal to you. I think the time has come when you must be made to realise you can't do as you like with me any more. Some men don't care to be made to look like fools.'

'I've never tried to do that,' she protested wildly. 'A lot of things which have happened in the past have been your own fault! Well—initially your own fault.'

'Thanks at least for that,' Brad responded dryly.

To her surprise he said no more, and she found herself too upset by the memories which kept crowding back to continue the argument. Which was all they ever seemed to do! Unhappily aware of this, she stared out of the window, the darkness through the glass having a strangely therapeutic effect. Drowsily her heavy eyelids closed and she slept.

When she woke the car had stopped; she was also aware of someone watching her. Brad? Through a haze of sleep his beloved face hovered above her. Still only half conscious, she raised her hand, to make sure he wasn't part of the dream she had just had. He had figured in it very largely.

He took her hand, in an odd moment which spelled tenderness. She thought she caught a fleeting glimpse of it on his mouth and in his eyes before it was lost in the familiar mockery.

'Wake up,' he said slowly. 'We've arrived.'

'So soon?' Still partially in her dream world, she went on searching his eyes, for what she thought she had seen there. Then, as a flash of light played over his face, intuition warned her that they hadn't arrived at Little Wrighton. Something was different.

'Where are we?' Alarm cleared her brain instantly as she struggled up.

'London.'

'London?' she echoed blankly. 'But why?'

'Why not?' A faintly derisive smile touched his mouth as he noted her alarm. 'I have a meeting here tomorrow, and saw no sense in going all the way to Derby, just to have to turn round and come practically straight back.'

Tightening her fingers to prevent a sharp panic increasing, Julie met his enigmatical eyes. 'You mentioned you had a flat?'

'I had,' releasing her seat belt, he took no notice of the quick breath she drew, 'but the lease came up three weeks ago, and I didn't renew it. I thought the time had come to have a family house. This one, in Knightsbridge, seems to fit the bill nicely. Plenty of room for a wife and any number of children.'

Julie could feel he was taunting her, and turned her hot face from him. The house looked attractive, she could see that from here, but she wasn't convinced she would ever live in it. Three weeks ago, he said, yet she hadn't been consulted, which was typical of their relationship from the beginning. Brad never consulted her on anything of importance. Sometimes he appeared to think she was too young to have any worthwhile opinions of her own.

It was dark and quiet, in what she vaguely recognised as one of London's most fashionable areas. Leaving the car, Brad took her in through a side door. From it they went up a short flight of steps, through another door into a narrow hall. From this a stairway curved graciously to the floor above.

To the right and left, he indicated the lounge and dining room, the adjoining kitchen. The decor was modern and tasteful, but the colours were rather faded.

As Julie gazed about her he asked softly, 'Do you like it? I took it over from some friends, as it stood. It needs redecorating and probably refurnishing, but I'll leave that to you.'

'It's very nice.' Shame made her swallow twice before she was able to reply. Brad was watching her very intently, as though it might really matter to him what she thought. Her conscience forced her to add, 'It looks charming as it is.'

The look on his face hardened as her efforts failed to cover her unease, as her eyes became fixed on the kitchen door. 'Are you looking for something in particular? Or— someone?'

The harshness of his voice warned her that he knew what she had on her mind, but it had to be said. 'Most men in your position have a housekeeper.'

'I haven't. At least, not yet.'

Anger flared with panic, as he so clearly ridiculed her mounting apprehension. 'That settles it, then!' Deliberately she spoke with sharp brashness. 'I can't stay here.'

His contemptuous shrug told her exactly what he thought of that, even as he said coldly, 'Don't be ridiculous, Julie.'

'I'm not being—ridiculous!' Her voice creaked and she tried to control it. 'You must see ... I know this isn't the village, but I expect people still talk.'

'Oh, God,' he sighed, 'surely not that, from you, of all people? We've surely travelled a long way from that particular hurdle, Julie. It's not as if you were an innocent young girl any more.'

'So you keep on asserting.' Hurt rioting through her, she couldn't find the spirit to challenge him further. Never could she match the strength of his vitality, which made him so alive and alert at any time of the day. At night, too, she thought, with a suddenly hammering pulse.

'All you ever tried to do was confirm my suspicions,' Brad snapped, 'so it's no use standing there trying to look hurt and untouched. One of these days I intend shattering that impression of cool innocence once and for all.'

With a strangled gasp she turned from him, knowing that if she tried to speak she might break down. After a moment she managed to murmur, 'Whatever you say, you can't force me to stay.'

'Come in here.' Without gentleness he took her arm, thrusting her before him to a moderately sized kitchen. Letting go of her, he picked up a kettle which he filled and switched on. 'We'll have a cup of tea while you tell me why you won't allow me the same privileges that you granted, or very nearly granted, Rodney Green.'

Feeling sick, Julie sagged against the table. 'Rodney wasn't like that!'

'You speak as though I'd hurt you, and I'm not talking of your arm.'

'You don't seem to care whether you do or not.'

Brad spooned tea, with annoying competence, into an old brown teapot. 'Would it help if I told you to stop worrying? So near our wedding, I don't intend anticipating it, but I suppose you'll still lie awake all night with your eyes fixed on the bedroom door. What will be in them, I wonder?' he taunted. 'Hope or fear?'

'You're despicable!' she breathed, brokenly. 'How can I trust you?'

Pouring water over the tea-leaves took only seconds. Leaving it to brew, Brad came around the table, jerking Julie into his arms. 'There are other things I want from you more than that.'

She was conscious of a melting sensation inside her as his dark eyes riveted on her, travelling slowly, lingering on the perfect shape of her. He made her so conscious of being a woman that she trembled—trembled and wanted to do nothing else but cling, as his head lowered and he kissed her. She might have surrendered, even as she guessed this was what he was deliberately trying to bring about, if his mouth had been kinder. But as he plundered unmercifully, with no regard for her tearful uncertainty, anger gave her the strength to wrench herself from his arms.

Stumbling back, she attempted to put some small distance between them, but he made no effort to follow her up. His eyes smouldered as she put trembling fingers to her mouth, but that was all. Grimly he said, 'Do you think I enjoy the way you flinch every time I come near you? After we're married there'll be no more of that!'

His face looked sombre and remote in spite of the purpose and intensity in his voice. Julie blinked and swallowed hard, flinching away from him again, as though her body was tuned to every hard cadence in his tones. 'No doubt you look forward to inflicting new tortures!'

His eyes narrowed. 'I asked you before and didn't get a straight answer. You seem to be implying that I'm capable of hurting you.'

Watching him pour the strong tea with steady hands, Julie wished she had even a little of his control. 'You do, sometimes, but I'm probably not the only one who has suffered.'

He pushed a full cup towards her over the table, 'There have been other women, but not one of them's ever complained.'

'Some will put up with anything.' She took a quick gulp of tea, feeling it warming her. The room felt warm.

'The heating's on?' She frowned slowly, feeling this should tell her something. Raising her eyes from her cup, she met Brad's.

'There's a caretaker, of sorts. I give him a ring when I'm coming and he does what's necessary. Does that answer your question?'

'I suppose so.' Resolutely she carried her empty cup to

the sink. 'It won't make me agree to stay, though. He won't sleep on the premises?'

'No—why should he?' Suddenly he seemed very tired of the subject. 'As for staying, you have no other option, so, if you feel troubled about it, console yourself with that.'

The water came out piping hot, when she turned on the tap to rinse her cup. Brad was determined she should stay. No amount of argument was going to move him. She could only pray that, if she waited patiently, she might get a chance to elude him. She was willing to try anything, anything but hitting him over the head again. Nothing would ever induce her to repeat that!

Lifting her head, she found him regarding her contemplatively. 'Would you like to go out for dinner?'

'Is there any alternative!' The effort to keep her voice even proved almost physical, but he must never guess how anxious she felt.

'We could stay in. Willow promised to put something in the fridge for me. Probably only steak, so you'd better think carefully.'

'What about you?'

'Julie!'

'Oh, all right,' she said hastily, 'we'll stay in. I expect you intended to, anyway, if you asked—Willow, did you call him, to get something in?'

'That's better.' He sounded relieved at her good sense.

Julie tried to go on being sensible. 'If you've a meeting in the morning, you must have notes to check. You could always do that while I cook the steak, and decide what I'm going to do.'

'You'll do exactly as I say, my girl.' Moving abruptly, he had a look of grim determination on his face as he glanced at the clock, 'No more running away, or trying to knock me senseless. So be warned!'

As she flushed, her eyes flying to the faint scar on his brow, he drew her firmly from the kitchen, up the stairs.

'I'll show you your room first. I don't know about you, but I'm having a shower before I do anything more. I feel filthy.'

Julie's mouth twisted wryly. Brad always looked immaculate, all six feet of him, well groomed. Sometimes, she thought, if she could have just one wish, it would be to be able to sit looking at him, for as long as she liked.

Obediently she followed him along the corridor on the next floor, into a small bedroom. 'Mine's next door and much larger,' he said dryly, 'should you feel like sharing.'

All the time Julie bathed and dressed, she wondered how she was going to escape undetected. She put on a pale rose-coloured dress with long sleeves, which was very flattering to her small waist and rounded hips and breasts. Her silky hair, which glinted like pale gold under the lights, she piled high on her small head, where it would be out of the way while she did the cooking. While congratulating herself that the style was severe enough to curb any man's desire, she didn't see how it exposed the bare loveliness of her nape, making her look curiously vulnerable.

As she slid a pinky lipstick over the tender contours of her mouth, she thought her chance to get away might come after Brad went to his study. Somewhere, at some time during the evening, there was bound to be an opportunity, and she must be ready to take it.

Downstairs, she found a large white apron, which covered her almost completely. She was just popping the steak under the grill when Brad appeared.

'Good girl,' he said approvingly. 'I think I could eat an elephant.'

'Which makes a change,' she quipped, 'from the usual horse!'

Gravely he considered this. 'I've always refused to say that. As a child I was extremely fond of horses.'

'Aren't you now?'

'Didn't you know I have two at Haydon?'

It was incredible that Brad and she should be teasing

each other lightly like this! Resolutely she stiffened from the enticing charm of him. 'I can't find any vegetables.'

'Here,' he produced tins and packages, 'dried potatoes, or whatever you call them, and peas. Carrots, too. We shouldn't starve.'

'You'd better open the tins, while I make a sauce. There's enough butter.'

For a few minutes they worked in harmony, Julie marvelling that it should be so. The rapport they had once known was back, and her throat choked with tears as she realised how much she had missed it. Before, though, there had been no pain, no unhappiness to eat the very heart from one's body.

Brad, who had set out mats and cutlery on the kitchen table, where they had elected to dine, released a satisfied sigh and said, 'Right! Let's eat.'

He poured wine in their glasses and the food tasted good. Julie, removing her apron, sustained the shock of his glance, which was disconcertingly frank. It rather rocked her newly found reassurance, but she tried to convince herself she had only imagined the rekindled smoulder at the back of his eyes.

Afterwards she made coffee, while Brad put cups on a tray, which he carried to the lounge. Later, replete with wine and coffee, she lay back in her chair. She had refused brandy with her coffee; she wasn't used to it and wanted to keep a clear head. She trusted the glint in Brad's eye no more than her own traitorous senses, and uneasily she suspected he was aware of how she felt towards him, how his kisses affected her.

The lounge was comfortable, but she couldn't relax. Brad seemed to do this easily as he drank his coffee, idly surveying her over the rim of his cup, as she tried to pretend she was thinking of nothing, while all the time she was juggling in her mind with taxis and trains, or, failing these, some hotel where she could spend the night.

At last, unable to bear the silence any longer, she asked

tentatively, 'Aren't you going to get on with whatever it is you have to check for your meeting tomorrow? I don't mind staying here by myself.'

'Ah, yes.' With an apparently reluctant sigh, Brad rose. 'Thanks for reminding me, I'd almost forgotten. I'd better go to the study. Would you like the TV?'

'TV?' for a moment she stared at him blankly. 'Oh, no, thank you. Besides, I don't know what's on. I'll just have a look at these,' she gestured to some magazines which lay on a low table.

Brad didn't argue. 'Just as you like.' He nodded briefly as he left her, as if it mattered little to him what she did while he was gone.

For a long while after he had left Julie sat watching the door. She wasn't foolish enough to imagine he wouldn't suspect she might try to run away. On the other hand, if he really did believe she was an experienced woman, he might think she was quite willing to stay, in spite of her protests.

Restlessly Julie sighed, trying hard to sort out her muddled thoughts. That Brad had brought her here this evening didn't necessarily mean he intended making love to her. It would have been a waste of time to have gone all the way to Derby when he had to be here tomorrow morning. And it was obviously her own fault that they hadn't stayed at his grandmother's and made an early start. Wasn't it time she stopped being so old-fashioned? Why didn't she pick up a magazine and go to bed, after locking her bedroom door? The lock looked strong enough; she had examined it earlier. If she couldn't trust Brad she could certainly trust that.

The coffee was cold and tasted bitter, like the taste in her mouth as she knew the arguments she waged with herself were no good. They made no impression on her welling fears. She must go! The risk of staying had been weighed so often against that of going that she could barely think straight. If she tried to escape and failed it would arouse Brad's anger, for she sensed he disliked the slightly melodramatic turn their affairs had taken. He hadn't said so outright, but she sensed his patience was growing thin.

Distraught, Julie got up at last, and went quickly to the door. The hall was quiet. Suddenly she realised Brad's study must be on the next floor as all the doors on this floor could be accounted for.

With a trembling sigh of relief she reached for her coat, which was still where she had left it over a chair. Checking that she had her handbag, she ran to the front door. She wasn't, after all, refusing to marry Brad; she was simply refusing to risk spending the night with him beforehand.

It seemed too good to be true that the elegant door opened to the touch, and that no stringent voice commanded her to come back as she let herself out into the cool, starry night. Gratefully she turned her hot face up to the skies, as her hand groped to pull the door to behind her.

'Going somewhere?'

'You ...!'

'Don't look so horror-stricken, Julie. I warned you against running away, for your own good.'

Julie, her legs suddenly weak, her pulse rate competing for an Olympic medal, found it difficult to speak as Brad's tall figure loomed above her. Where had he been? What was he doing out here? 'You've been spying on me!' she gasped.

'Come, Julie,' he sounded weary rather than terribly angry, 'I think I've had enough of this kind of thing to last me a lifetime. Do we have to play it out to the bitter end?'

'I don't know what you mean!' she hedged round the truth, 'but you can't stop me from going.'

Again the bitter twist to his mouth. 'I don't let women roam around London at this time of night on their own. No guest of mine.'

His voice had an icy edge to it and his eyes were as cold. She looked at him helplessly, cold herself, except for her arm, where the grip of his steely fingers whipped spirals of burning flames. 'It's not yet eleven.'

'Late enough, and you're a pretty girl. Come on, back inside.'

She paused, looking up at him, conscious of his hand sliding to her waist, forcing her to obey whether she wished to or not. All her wishes were of no avail against such physical strength.

Able to read no sign of relenting on his face, she whispered helplessly, 'I'm sorry ...'

'You might be.'

What threat lay behind those few idle words? 'Brad——' as a quiver of fear leapt, she flinched, 'I—if I'd managed to get home tonight, I was still going to marry you.'

'Good of you,' he jeered curtly, and thrust her aside to secure the door.

He turned and her heart missed a beat as she felt his contempt, as she became aware of anger smouldering deep inside him, something she had missed outside. Wildly, she began, 'I know you have no great opinion of either Joe or me, but I promise I'll manage to pay back that money some day. If Joe doesn't, I will, no matter what I have to do.'

'Forget it,' he said tightly. 'Now get back to the lounge while I make some tea. You look as though you could do with bed and something stronger, but on both counts I expect I'd be wrong.'

When he returned with the tea Julie had taken off her coat and sat on her chair again, her mind emptied of all further thoughts of defiance. It was as though he had at last drained her resistance. There remained only a strange urge to please him which she found not unpleasant.

As he drew nearer, to give her her tea, and her eyes met his fully, her heart began racing as she tried to interpret his black, smouldering gaze. She felt an ache go right through her body, as if he held her and kissed her, and only just was she able to murmur a husky word of thanks for her tea and look away.

She didn't notice that he didn't have any, nor did she notice that he perceived how her hands shook, so very badly that he waited until she drained her cup, then took it from her.

'Feeling better?'

'Yes.'

As he placed the cup on the table, she heard the breath being drawn deeply into his lungs. 'Where did you intend going?'

'I wasn't sure.' Her head drooped unhappily, her once neat coiffure straggling untidily over her cheeks. 'Home, I suppose.'

'Is it as bad as all that?'

Some note in his voice which sounded incredibly like compassion stirred her. Unpredictable tears sprang to her eyes and, as she groped for a handkerchief, Brad uttered something under his breath and drew her quickly up beside him.

'Julie?' he put his hands on her waist, drawing her to him. Putting a hand under her chin, he lifted her face, meeting her tear-drenched eyes. Above her, his strong features swam darkly and she could feel the strength of his hands holding her immobile.

'Julie,' he said thickly, 'I don't want to feel I'm making you do things against your will. I have my troubles, too, you know. Nothing's as clear as I would like it to be, but there's no need for you to be—unhappy.'

She drew a deep breath, lowering her lashes to hide her love for him. 'I don't think I'm that any more.'

'Well then ...?'

Her heart leapt at the suddenly warm feeling in his voice, as he sensed the responsive change in her. She realised she knew more of her feelings than she had supposed. He knew, all right, that she was vulnerable where he was concerned; knew how she ached for him—with desire ...

'Brad,' she whispered, as his lips found hers.

It was a long, sweet kiss, filled with passion. He kissed

her until she was breathless, their bodies close against each other. He seemed intent on draining every ounce of sweetness from her lips, and she responded unresistingly to the urgency of his hands and mouth.

If before she had any doubts about it, she had none now. Brad kissed her as if she was a woman, a desirable one, whom he wasn't merely playing with any more. Her whole body burned and shuddered within the agonising pressure of his arms.

At last he raised his head, turning his face against her hair. His mouth moved in the soft fragrance of it, breathing deeply. 'It's beautiful—you're beautiful.'

The words were low-spoken, but their very intensity was intoxicating. Brad had kissed her as though he meant it, and no man could have spoken like that insincerely. Julie wanted to say something in response, but frightened of breaking the spell, she buried her face soundlessly in the silky front of his shirt. Against her cheek his heart thundered heavily, seemingly a confirmation of her own wild longing.

Without speaking he kissed her again, murmuring against her ear, his hands caressing her, his lips on her mouth, her eyelids, her throat, until she felt sick with desire and her senses reeled.

Long moments later he said hoarsely, 'Julie, stay with me tonight.'

CHAPTER TEN

'STAY with you?' Julie should have felt shocked, but she was beyond that. There was no place for it in the warm yearning world she inhabited. There was only Brad and the senuous passion he was making no attempt now to disguise, his voice alive with determined persuasion.

'I want you,' he groaned, 'I've always wanted you. I've told you before, but not how much. Since the first time I saw you. Tonight—you must ...'

She wanted him, too. She knew it now. Wanted him too desperately to take any notice of the small voice of warning. Yet she tried. 'I can't, Brad. Please, no!'

'Why not? You want me, I can feel it.'

'To You.' She was somewhere past pretending. She had only to look at him, meet the indisputable power in his eyes, to be lost. Bitterly she was conscious of her own weakness, yet ready to glory in it. Ready to give herself to him without any guarantee for the future. It seemed the measure of her love that it no longer recognised any barriers. No longer did it demand absolute security before full commitment. She was ready to give and give, for as long as Brad wanted her ...

He was saying softly, not yet aware of her surrender, 'I could make you, you know.'

'You don't have to.' Her voice came low and broken, for she would be giving something she had held sacred. Her lips parted as he bent to them, but in her face he could read only the essence of desire.

'Come with me, upstairs,' he said arrogantly, very sure now of his power. 'You won't regret it.'

Held high in his arms, Julie wasn't conscious of him taking her to his room. Sliding her to the floor, he was won-

drously gentle as he began slowly to undress her. Expertly
his fingers dealt with the zip of her dress, her half slip,
then the fastening on her bra. She heard his breath rasp
and his half groan as he buried his lips deeply in her warm
flesh. She could feel the movement of his mouth against
her heartbeat, his hands curling tightly on her waist, bending her forcibly back to him as the strength of his feelings
rose swiftly into urgent passion.

'Julie,' he murmured thickly, 'Julie ...'

Naked in his arms, she couldn't stop him from doing
what he liked with her. His hands searched intimately over
her, caressing, exploring, arousing her until her emotions
were out of control. Her body seemed to be floating, burning in space, yearning towards some distant goal which
was coming dazzlingly nearer, but which she knew hazily
would shatter her completely.

Against her thigh the hardness of his muscles was beginning to hurt, and while she was dimly aware there could be
worse to come, she could only moan his name against the
sensuous pressure of his mouth. As he lifted her again and
eased himself over her, her fingers dug fiercely into the
smooth muscles of his broad back.

Then the telephone on the bedside cabinet rang. Brad
went tense, his hand leaving the taut curve of Julie's
breast as it kept on ringing, like a discordant note. Moments
later they might never have heard it. Even now, Julie
didn't stir, wishing, as she was to recall with shame, that
Brad would ignore it. Under his breath she heard him
mutter savagely, then there came a sigh of angry frustration.

'I'll have to see who it is, darling. I believe my grandmother is one of the few who have this number. It must be
her. No one else would ring me in the middle of the night.'

As he picked up the receiver, Julie made an effort to
free herself and turned away from him. Immediately she
missed the warmth of his body, but it wasn't wholly this
which made her feel suddenly cold. Brad Hewson had

raised her to the heights of an almost intolerable excitement, but it had only taken one small interruption to destroy the harmony between them, to expose the guilt which still lay under the passion which had so nearly overwhelmed her. Regret chilled her even while her cheeks flushed hotly with shame.

Brad's hand snaked out, as she would have left him, his tight clasp letting her know he wouldn't easily let her go. Her cheeks bright red, she steadily averted her eyes from his bare limbs as he spoke to his caller.

Only then did she begin to realise something was wrong. She had fancied, when Brad had mentioned his grandmother, that the old lady was just trying to satisfy her sharp curiosity—that she suspected they might be here and couldn't wait to find out. But the person on the line didn't sound like a woman, and Brad's voice was clipped, his answers brief, completely without expression of any kind.

He said, 'Yes, we'll come at once,' before putting down the receiver.

He sat for a second, brow creased, not moving, then letting go of her arm he threw Julie a wrap, almost in the same movement. The wrap was his, and while she struggled numbly into it he began buttoning his shirt up, but as though he wasn't completely conscious of what he was doing.

In spite of the thick silk dressing gown held closely around her, Julie shivered as she stared at his taut face. He had gone pale. The last time she had looked at him dazedly, his face had been slightly flushed, his mouth warm and moving with desire. Now his eyes were cold, the line of his strong jaw tight, his mouth grim.

'Brad?' she made a great effort to get past the sudden obstruction in her throat, 'is it—has something happened to your grandmother?'

'No.' He had got to his feet, but he dropped down beside her again, on the edge of the bed. 'I'm sorry, Julie,

I was thinking of something else, and it wasn't my grand-mother.'

What did he mean? He seemed stunned, as if he had been hit by more shocks than one, and for the first time in his life was confronted by something he wasn't sure how to cope with. Of course this couldn't be true, not of Brad Hewson. Julie could never imagine him being uncertain over anything!

'Brad?' she appealed anxiously, still unsteady from the force of his lovemaking.

Whatever it was that troubled him, apart from the news he had received, he put it quickly from him. 'Julie,' his gaze went tensely over her face as he took her hands in his, rubbing them softly, 'I wish I could spare you.'

The bad news must concern her. Fear moved through her. 'What is it?' she whispered, knowing now that her cold premonition hadn't been imagined. 'Who is it?' she amended apprehensively, as he still didn't speak. 'It—it can't be Joe?'

'It is.' For the second time that evening she saw com-passion in Brad's eyes, 'I'm afraid you're going to have to be strong, Julie. There's been a fire.'

'A fire?' Her eyes widened, horror coming quickly. 'Oh, no! Are you sure? Where was it—— Is he——?' Numb now, with a terrible despair, she couldn't actually put her fears in words. 'Was he ...?'

'Yes, Julie, I'm afraid so.' His voice was thin, as though the breaking of this, of the pain it must bring, was in-tolerable. 'That was the police I was speaking to. They traced us through my grandmother. Joe didn't stand a chance.'

Julie never forgot the horror, the remorse, the ensuing shock of the following hours. Brad helping her to dress because her hands trembled so, the packing of her few other clothes, the darkness of their journey back to Little Wrighton. Brad was there, supporting her, dealing with everything, but he could never remove that first appalled horror, nor take away the weight of guilt which beset her each time she wondered if she might not have been able to save Joe, had she been at home.

It was never proved exactly what had happened. A man going home late at night had seen smoke pouring out of a window, but Joe had been in bed, and before they reached him, it was too late. He had died from the fumes, shortly after being admitted to hospital.

Edith, after the funeral, announced that she was going to stay with her sister until after the Christmas holidays. Then she must find the courage to return to the village until she retired. Julie didn't press her as to her future plans, but as she said goodbye she promised to keep in touch. Joe's death had been a terrible blow to Edith, she could tell. It would take her a long time to get over it.

Brad insisted that Julie stay at Haydon Hill. Foster had an older sister, a trained cook, who was looking for work, and who agreed to come immediately. During the first terrible days Julie leant on Brad continually, finding she couldn't do without his rock-like strength, yet feeling completely remote. While she hadn't loved Joe dearly, she had been fond of him, and would never have wanted him to go as he had. When Brad told her that everyone at the works was sorry, she felt oddly grateful to him that Joe had died without anyone knowing he had sullied his good name.

The funeral was a large one and Julie wasn't aware of the many curious glances directed towards her as she stood forlornly in the exposed country churchyard, with Brad Hewson's tall figure shielding her from the late November rain. She was aware, though, that neither she nor Edith might have got through the day without him, and again came the gratitude which seemed to have nothing to do with love.

To Julie's astonishment Brad's grandmother arrived that same evening—without any invitation, Brad assured Julie, grimly, from him. Without taking any notice of his cool welcome, Mrs Hewson said she intended staying a few days. Surprisingly, she appeared to have changed her mind about Julie, for she was quite friendly and very kind. To Julie it didn't seem to matter any more, as she knew she must soon have things out with Brad. It wouldn't be possible to put off much longer.

The opportunity came sooner than she had expected, but strangely enough it was Brad who eventually sought her out, not the other way around. He called her to his study about a week later, one morning, when she thought he would have left for Derby. If Julie was looking slightly thinner and pale, so was he. Gazing at him anxiously, she saw that his face was strained, his mouth thinly held. How heartily tired he must have grown of—everything. What a trial this must have been for him. In a moment, when she offered him his freedom, how relieved he was going to be.

'Sit down, Julie.' Politely he pulled out a chair, his manner so strangely formal that she felt tears suddenly pricking her eyelids. The wind blew cold against the window, followed by a patter of grey rain, and inside her a bleak despair grew heavier.

Unable to raise a smile, she did as she was told, but outwardly, at least, managed to stay cool and composed. Because Brad had sent for her, she waited for him to speak first. It wasn't until he began that she realised, with a harsh sense of shock, he was suggesting exactly the same thing that she had been going to suggest herself—the ending of their engagement.

'All this business about Joe is over now, Julie, over and forgotten. I can't and I won't hold you to anything any longer. You know as well as I do that our engagement is a complete farce. I must have been mad to even think about it; crazy beyond understanding to go to the lengths I did.' He paused, she heard his breath drag as she stared down at her hands. 'You must be glad to know you're free.'

There was silence, as every word he uttered shocked.

Pain dragged through her like torture, so momentarily unbearable she had to bite her lips to prevent herself from crying out. She had been going to offer him his ring back, but this was altogether different. Yet she must say something; make some move if she didn't want him to guess how much she loved him. He must never do that!

'Yes, Brad.' Lifting a white face, she drew his ring from her finger, trying not to remember how very short a time it had been there. 'I—I was going to give you it back, in any case. I hoped you would take it, but it seems I needn't have worried. You must have guessed my feelings exactly.'

Accepting the ring, he dropped it quickly into a drawer in his desk, as if he never wanted to see it, or her, again. Closing the drawer, he hesitated suddenly, his dark brows drawn. Then, as if her white face goaded him beyond everything, he said harshly, 'You realise, I expect, that nothing happened that night in London? You still have your innocence.'

Again Julie lowered her head. A quiver ran through her, right through her breast, and she clenched her hands tightly to keep from trembling. Silently she nodded. He was obviously waiting for some kind of answer, but there were some things she wasn't yet able to talk about.

'Good,' she almost felt his sigh of relief, as he thankfully put that behind him. 'Do you want your old job back, Julie?'

'Oh, no. No, thank you.' It hurt, but she was grateful that he referred to the future, rather than the past, and to more impersonal things. 'I've been thinking about this, Brad. I heard of a firm in Derby who were looking for office staff last week, and I also know of a landlady who might just take me. A friend of mine lived with her for over a year, and she said if ever I want digs ...'

It was understood, without mentioning it, that she couldn't go back to the burnt-out house in the village. Even Joe's car, in the garage next to the house, had been destroyed, and there had been no insurance.

Julie was startled when Brad said tersely, 'You could always live here. My grandmother seems to have forgotten what's gone before. It never made any difference to me, but if it matters to you ...'

'No, Brad,' her voice was breaking and she rose quickly. 'It would never work—staying here, I mean. Your grandmother hasn't turned out to be an ogre. In fact, she's really a dear, when one gets to know her, but I couldn't stay here.'

'As you like.' She could feel him staring at her averted face, but he appeared not to notice her uncertainty, her craving to be taken into his arms, to hear him say he would never let her go, assurances which she knew he wasn't able to give. There was surely that in both his voice and manner which betrayed that he would be glad to see the last of her.

When she said no more, he walked past her to the door, his face absolutely expressionless. Politely, she thought, he murmured, 'Think about it, Julie. Don't do anything in a hurry. I'll see you later.'

Later, Julie decided, would be too late. She couldn't trust herself not to go down on her knees and beg. Beg for only what he had offered in the first place. Ask him, in utter humility, to never let her go. No, she couldn't risk that happening; she must hold on to her pride.

She must be gone before Brad returned. A full day lay ahead of her, but she had plenty of time, for he worked late in the evenings. Organising herself mentally, Julie rang the firm who had been advertising for secretarial staff, after finding the number in the directory. Fortunately she managed to get an appointment for the very next morning. Next she rang the landlady with whom her friend had stayed, and was lucky there too. Yes, she could come right away; Mrs Owen did have a room, Jane's room, which Mrs Owen hadn't intended re-letting, but she remembered Julie and wouldn't mind her having it. After that, with the reckless feeling that she might as well plunge in at the deep end, Julie rang for a taxi. On the table beside the telephone she placed a pound for her phone calls. It was pitifully little, considering the expense Brad must have been put to over the past week, but it did seem a beginning. In the note which she also left she promised to repay every penny she and Joe owed, or die in the attempt.

When Mrs Hewson came down shortly afterwards, Julie told her she was going.

'Going where, child?'

Her face white again, Julie explained, 'Brad and I aren't getting married, after all. Brad—that is we decided we weren't suited, but he didn't ask me to go. This is my decision . . .'

All the way to Derby Julie kept recalling, with some surprise, Mrs Hewson's dismay. In other circumstances Julie might have felt flattered. At first Mrs Hewson had flatly refused to believe it. Even yet Julie wasn't sure if she had managed to convince her. As she left, the old lady had been threatening to ring Brad.

Julie could never remember feeling so alone as she did during the first days at her new job. The firm wasn't large, but it was very successful, and she was offered the post of assistant to the managing director's secretary—this, apparently, on the strength of the glowing recommendation they had received from Miss Harrison. Julie, who didn't consider herself all that good, was grateful and vowed to do her best to live up to it. This she managed to do easily, as she allowed herself to think of nothing but work.

At first she had thought Brad might try to contact her, especially as she had left in such a hurry, but he didn't. The nights were the worst, when she found herself thinking of him until the pain grew unbearable. Then she would get up, anguish almost blinding her, to sit by her window looking out at the night sky, staring at the blur of city lights under the twinkling stars until her body was as cold as her heart.

It was this inability to forget, in the quietness of her

room, which led her to accept an invitation. She missed Joe; missed her home in the village, but it was nothing to the desolation she knew when she thought of Brad. One or two of the younger men in the firm, quick to notice her young, appealing beauty, had asked her out, but she had always refused. After knowing Brad, she was aware that friendship was all she could ever offer other men and, for many, she realised this would not be enough. These days, very few men took a girl out without expecting, at least, some fairly intimate kisses, and this she knew she could never consent to, or endure, not loving Brad Hewson the way she did.

But when the managing director of the firm asked her out, she scarcely felt herself in a position to refuse. Michael Wren was only in his early thirties, but he looked much older. Often he reminded Julie of the elderly uncle she had never had. He was so kindly and considerate, his warm patience a balm to a girl with an aching heart. Often Julie thought he looked oddly weary and was surprised to find herself once wishing she could soothe the lines of worry from his brow. Not that he had much to worry about, she supposed, as he owned the business and appeared to make enough money.

As assistant to his secretary, she naturally took over when Mrs Baker was ill. This was when Michael Wren invited her to go to a party with him. Mrs Baker had been away almost three weeks and Julie was becoming vaguely aware that he found her attractive. At first he hadn't seemed to notice her, but this had changed. Now she found him watching her occasionally, with an expression in his eyes she found very disconcerting. It was at times like this when she suddenly found herself wishing hopelessly that she had never met and learnt to love a man she must forget.

When Michael asked her out, he was quick to notice her uncertainty. 'It's a cousin of mine,' he explained, hastily, as though to reassure her. 'She gives this do every year and gets tired of me turning up alone. This year she insists

I bring a partner, I suppose to save her the trouble of looking for one for me.'

Julie couldn't help smiling faintly, at what she thought was a rather strange invitation. Didn't Michael Wren realise his own worth? Brad would have issued such an invitation like a command, taking care, of course, to lace it with his irresistible charm, but this man here—why, he sounded almost apologetic!

'I'm sure you wouldn't find it difficult to find someone to go with you, Mr Wren. Any girl ...'

'But I don't want—just any girl,' his plain but pleasant face became surprisingly stubborn, 'I'm asking you.'

Quite suddenly Julie agreed, feeling it might be easier to say yes than to listen to more persuasions, which could only detract from the dignity of them both. Besides, she hadn't a valid excuse for refusing, not one she could give. She couldn't very well say, 'I'm sorry I can't go with you, Mr Wren, as I happen to be desperately in love with another man.'

She was forced to go out and buy a new dress as the only long ones she had were the ones Brad had bought for her, and these she had left at Haydon Hill. All her other clothes had been burnt in the fire. The one which she purchased for the party was white, a colour she had always looked well in, but, apart from the colour, it had little to recommend it. There was another which she liked much better, but at double the price she didn't even allow herself to consider it. It was imperative she save as much as she could to pay Brad back, and, at the rate she was going, after she had kept herself there was little enough left. Certainly not enough to splash out on an expensive dress which she might never wear again.

When she was ready, however, she felt better. With her hair newly shampooed and shining, and the pale material of her dress lending her flawless skin a silky sheen, she knew she need not have worried about letting Michael down. As she heard his car and went down to join him, she was startled to find how relieved she was at the prospect of escaping for a few hours from her own company. Michael Wren's undemanding presence loomed like an oasis in the sandy desert of her own thoughts.

He hadn't said that his cousin was married to one of Brad Hewson's best friends, or Julie would never have gone. The expression on Michael's pleasant face had been disquieting enough, when he had first seen her that evening, but to see Brad walk into the sumptuous house, with a woman clinging to his arm, made her feel faint, as waves of sickness rose from her stomach. It took her all her time to beat it back; to remain by Michael's side and not rush out.

Brad paused, speaking to his host. Julie stared at him, unable to help it. Unconsciously she was grateful that she was shaded by a huge, decorative palm, so he didn't see her straight away. He looked as tough and imposing as ever, undeniably attractive in his dark dinner jacket, but his face seemed tired. Too many office parties, she supposed, too many late nights, or—her heart knew a terrible pain as she gazed at the clinging woman by his side—too many 'all nights', more likely! The voluptuous woman who was with him would want a demanding lover.

It was at that moment, as he glanced in her direction, that their eyes met. Even at this distance his surprise was unmistakable and reminded Julie instantly of another dinner party at the Green's, when she had experienced that same coldness. For a moment she fancied he was disconcerted, but if he had been it could have nothing to do with her. She saw his mouth harden as his glance flicked to Michael Wren, and she flushed as it returned to her with derision. Unable to retain his grim stare, she wrenched her own eyes away, knowing that never before had she hit such a depth of despair.

Much later, after they had dined and Michael had torn himself from her for a duty dance with their hostess, she found Brad beside her. He didn't ask her to dance and her body was so rigid she was glad. All evening he had given no sign of recognition, and she had begun to believe he didn't intend to. Now to find him here was a shock which she found almost impossible to hide.

'You haven't wasted much time!' His words came low but with such deadly emphasis that she shrank.

'Good evening, Brad.' Deciding she must ignore his sarcasm, she tried to speak coolly, but her voice came in a frightened little gasp.

As if she hadn't spoken, he added coldly, 'He seems quite struck on you—hasn't taken his eyes off you all night and sticks by you like a jailer!'

As this, unhappily, was Julie's own impression, she didn't attempt to deny it, but she did say sharply, as anger stirred at his offensive tones, 'Mr Wren is very kind.'

'Oh, come off it, Julie!' His laughter was harsh. 'I've known Michael Wren for years. He's kind and he's also rich!'

'What's that got to do with it?'

'As to that, I'll arrive at the answer if you give me a moment. You don't love him—so it must be the money. Money you would like to use to repay me. It's taken me about all evening, but I think I have it worked out!'

'Really, Brad,' Julie's blue eyes sparked with controlled hysteria, 'you do put ideas in my head!'

'There's plenty of space,' he returned insultingly, his voice grating with underlying fury. 'But let me warn you, Julie, if you turn up at Haydon dangling Wren's cheque, I'll put the bloody thing in the fire!'

'How dare you!' She felt in a fever and forgot to lower her voice. Then, as her glance swivelled wildly, she saw heads turning and heard Brad's lady friend call. 'You'd better go,' she sneered bitterly, meeting his icy eyes. 'Your jailer, this time!'

'At least she's more generous than you were,' he replied insolently, turning away.

As Michael Wren stopped outside her digs, he said

tentatively, 'I'd no idea you knew Brad Hewson.'

'I——' she might as well tell him, things had a peculiar way of getting out, 'We were engaged, once.'

'You and Hewson?' She wasn't looking at him, but she rather fancied he reeled with shock. 'I did hear something about an engagement, but I had no idea it was you.'

'We weren't engaged long.'

'Perhaps I shouldn't have mentioned him,' Michael frowned. 'It was just that you seemed so shaken after he spoke to you, tonight. I'd hate to feel responsible for letting him hurt you.' He stared at her closely, until she began to feel uncomfortable under his intent gaze. 'I'm beginning to realise this would hurt me as much as it might hurt you.'

The growing certainty that Michael Wren was falling in love with her, and because of this she must soon have to find another job, added to the general depression which plagued Julie for the rest of the week. Even to think of having a deeper relationship with another man, loving Brad the way she did, was impossible. Once Brad had asked her to live with him and she had turned him down. She had felt it right to do so at the time, but she hadn't loved him then as she did now. If he was to ask her again she knew she wouldn't have the strength to refuse him. What comfort was pride, she thought dismally, when one had nothing else but that left?

To Julie's surprise, on Friday evening, when she got back to her digs, there was a message from Mrs Hewson, asking if she would come to tea the following afternoon at Haydon. Mr Hewson was away for the weekend, Julie's landlady repeated the message faithfully, and Mrs Hewson was lonely.

Feeling it would be churlish to refuse, as Mrs Hewson had been so kind to her after Joe had died, Julie rang Foster and told him she would be there, if the snow which was forecast didn't arrive to stop her. She wouldn't have gone if Brad had been at home. As it was, she decided, she would only stay an hour.

Even an hour might be too long. Doubtfully, Julie gazed around her at the snow which had began falling since she got off the bus. The ground was dry and it soon lay thickly, coating the surrounding countryside like icing sugar.

At Haydon she knocked several times, but no one came. Eventually she tried the door. She nearly turned away, until she remembered Mrs Hewson was a little deaf and Foster could be out somewhere. Besides, Mrs Hewson surely wouldn't have sent for her unless it had been about something important?

There was no one in the hall, or the drawing room, when she looked in there. Remembering how they had all made shameless use of Brad's cosy study, she turned rather nervously in that direction. Mrs Hewson must be there, probably having a nap. Ladies of her advanced age often did.

Opening the door, she started back, as though a bomb had exploded under her feet. It wasn't Mrs Hewson who sat sleeping in the chair before the fire, but Brad! He was lounging against the leather upholstery, looking curiously weary, but immediately she made a sound he opened his eyes, and she realised he hadn't been sleeping at all.

'Julie!' With a sharp exclamation he was on his feet, betraying that he was just as surprised as she. 'I might have been thinking of you,' he said brusquely, 'but you're the last person I expected to see.' His mouth hardened at the unconscious dismay on Julie's paling face. 'As you apparently came on your own accord, I don't know why you should look so shocked. You've always known I lived here.'

The impact of his presence was so shattering that her voice didn't easily function. 'I—your grandmother asked me to come for tea. I didn't want to, but I felt I should.' That took so much effort, Julie felt she had been running. 'She—she said you were away.'

'So I was,' he rejoined grimly, coming swiftly towards her, to cut off an instinctive retreat. 'Now that you're this far, there's no sense in running away as though I were going to eat you. Come and sit down.'

She obeyed, feeling suddenly too weak to do anything else, but sat on the very edge of her chair.

He sat opposite, his regard steady, his eyes dark. 'Well?'

'I——' she began stammering, then tried again. 'You must believe I wouldn't have come, if I'd known you were to be—to be ...'

'Here?' he finished, as she faltered unhappily. 'Why not?'

Defencelessly she stared at the carpet, 'Well, I——' furtively she licked dry lips, 'I didn't think you would want to see me.'

'How do you know?' he muttered tautly. Then, as she just shook her head wordlessly, 'My grandmother isn't here. She probably intended to be, but she had an urgent call from Sussex this morning. Some squabble among the staff.' His broad shoulders lifted. 'Apparently her housekeeper threatened to leave, so she immediately ordered Foster to drive her home. He won't return until tomorrow, maybe later, if the weather worsens, but I can always make you a cup of tea.'

Julie swallowed, knowing she couldn't bear to stay another minute. 'I'm sorry to have missed your grandmother, Brad, but I think it would be better if I left.'

Harsh lines drew his mouth thinly, as she stood up. 'You can't go without something.'

'No, honestly, I'll be all right.'

'Please yourself!'

As though he couldn't now wait to be rid of her, he took an abrasive stride towards the door.

'Brad?' She tried to summon enough pride to propel her past him, but failed. By her sides, her hands hung limply, her legs refusing to obey the urgent message from her brain. Mutely she groped for a few sensible words of farewell, but none came. Her face far more eloquent than she ever knew, she could only whisper his name, 'Brad ...'

Suddenly it was as if something within him snapped. He was back by her side, pulling her roughly into his arms, his eyes glittering, leaping with flames of urgent desire. 'Julie! Oh, God, Julie, don't you know how much I love you, how much I care?' His voice was muffled against her silky hair and she couldn't believe she had heard aright.

'Brad?' There was anguish in her voice, in the wide suffering of the eyes she raised helplessly to his. 'Please don't tease me. You can't possibly love me!'

He stared down at her, while her heart beat painfully, unable to believe the agony she saw on his face. 'But I do,' he groaned thickly, as his mouth lowered to crush her parted lips. 'Oh, Julie—I do, I do!'

How long they stood there, she had no idea. All she was conscious of was their hungry, aching passion, the tightness of her own clinging arms, Brad's seemingly irrevocable intention never to let her go again.

While they murmured their love for each other, he picked her up and carried her to the sofa, where hazily she supposed it had all begun. There he went on kissing her, his mouth going passionately over the vulnerable hollows of her face and throat, until there was no area of resistance left in her soft, yielding body. The sensual force of his mouth provoked a storm of response. Julie felt a wild excitement replacing the flood of gratitude which surged through her veins, the incredulous gratitude she had known when he told her he loved her. Now it appeared this love was overwhelming him with an insatiable desire to get as close as possible without actually possessing her. His arms tightened painfully, and the blinding rush of emotion left her quivering and spent. Then, as if he could trust himself no longer, he put her gently away from him.

When he brushed back her tumbled hair softly, so he could see her face, she whispered tremulously, 'I love you, Brad. I don't think I realised how much until recently, but nothing else seems to matter any more. A few minutes ago I was going to offer to live with you, with or without your love.' Brokenly, she added, 'Now it seems as though a miracle has happened.'

'Hush,' he said, bending to kiss her mouth gently. 'We're going to be married, tomorrow if possible. I still have a licence. You aren't the only one who's been hoping for a miracle, you know.'

She had to ask, 'How—when did you know you loved me?'

His smile was bitter, momentarily taking the happiness from his face. 'I've been a fool, Julie. It wasn't until I heard about the fire. It wasn't until then, when it came to me that you could easily have been in the house with Joe, that I realised how much I loved you. It wasn't until then that I knew what was keeping me awake at nights; what was keeping you so continually in my thoughts, so I could think of little else. Why my secretary had to catch me doodling your face at board meetings, where I should certainly have been thinking of something else. I'm ashamed to say I thought it was merely a stronger version of the usual desire, and to be satisfied in the same way.'

'But you never actually did,' Julie breathed.

His mouth twisted ruefully, 'I have to confess I came near to it, darling. With you my control was never what it should have been. But the only time my intentions might have been deliberate was after you hit me over my head. For a few hours after I came around, my temper was such that, had I been able, I would have extracted the most primitive revenge!'

'Oh, Brad!' Helpless to show her remorse in any other way, Julie put her arms impulsively round his waist, laying her head against his shoulder. 'I felt terrible about that! Nothing seemed to be going right. I'd never been so frightened in my life and didn't know what to do. Then you found out about Joe and forced me to agree to live with you. After that, when you asked me to marry you, after finding me with Rodney, I felt worse than ever.'

'How do you think I felt?' As if to punish her he tugged

a strand of shining hair sharply. 'I knew I was wrong to blackmail you regarding Joe, but I thought if I didn't resort to desperate measures I would lose you. You never knew, did you,' he asked dryly, 'how I went out that afternoon and bought the most expensive ring I could find? Not with love in my heart, I'm afraid, my darling, but determination that if it was marriage you wanted, then you should have it! But I suspected, even then, that I was trying to fool myself. Then, when I couldn't find you at home and, after searching, found you in that bedroom with young Green, I could have cheerfully killed you. It did, however, provide the excuse I was looking for, enabling me to have you and save my pride at the same time—or so I thought.'

'Then my ring wasn't a—a family heirloom?'

'No,' he said wryly, 'but you know why I had to pretend it was?' Turning her flushed face up to his, he added with mock severity, 'Can you wonder that sometimes I imagined I disliked you very much? Because of you I found myself practising deceptions I would never have believed myself capable of. All the same,' he said, more soberly, 'I do realise I must have hurt you very much, and looking back, I wonder if you'll ever be able to forgive me.'

'Hush!' Julie whispered, love shining from her eyes as she laid a tender finger across his mouth. 'The past doesn't matter any more, just as long as we have each other.'

'No,' he agreed huskily, kissing the finger against his lips before bending again to her mouth. As her arms went tightly around his neck and he crushed her closer, for a long time there was silence. Lifting his head at last, he said softly against her warm cheek, 'I maybe didn't love you right away, but from the first time I saw you at the bus stop, Julie Gray, I fancied you!'

To hide the sudden tears of emotion in her eyes, she retorted pertly, 'You didn't look as if you ever had, when we met the other night!'

Brad's eyes glinted as he growled, 'Don't mention that!

I can assure you, my dear, that Michael Wren will be one of the first to learn of our marriage. I was out of my mind with jealousy. I scarcely slept that night, wondering if I'd lost you.'

'Yet it was you who sent me away in the first place,' Julie reminded him unevenly.

'Because I was seeing you through the eyes of a man who loved you.' His mouth tightened. 'I felt you must have a chance to see things clearly. That I had to give you time, without any strings attached, and there seemed only one way to do it. You don't know the misery I went through, abiding by that decision. Seeing you with Mike Wren made me feel quite savage, I can tell you.'

'You couldn't have felt more miserable than I did,' Julie gulped. 'There I was, loving you to distraction, and all you could do was shout!'

'I'm sorry,' he offered, looking anything but, his eyes exploring her mouth, his obvious intentions making her senses swim.

'Brad,' she said weakly, 'did you know I was to be here today?'

'No.' Momentarily he paused, smiling faintly. 'But I think my grandmother has been very crafty. She got in touch and said I must come back as there'd been a terrible crisis. Then she rang off, just like that. She wouldn't even answer when I tried to ring her back. Fortunately I was spending the weekend with an old friend and he excused my hasty departure. When I arrived here and found her note about some trival domestic disagreement, I didn't know what to make of it. Until you walked in.'

'Why should she go to so much trouble?'

'I suspect she was trying to put things right between us. I think she guessed how much I was suffering.'

'Oh, Brad!' There was such gratitude in Julie's heart, she felt overwhelmed. As Brad bent his head, with renewed purpose, she said quickly, 'Don't you think, as we owe her so much, that we should give her a ring? We can tell her how we've found each other again; how much we love each other.'

'Yes, perhaps we should.' Brad rose, drawing Julie up adoringly into the curve of his arm, and together they walked towards the telephone. 'I could also tell her that we'll come and spend another few days with her, after our honeymoon. Would you like that?'

'Oh, yes,' Julie breathed happily. 'Oh, yes please!' And she wasn't sure whether it was Brad's fault or her own that it was some time later before he got round to dialling his grandmother's number!

Romance novels that speak
the language of love known to
women the world over.

Harlequin Presents...

A distinctive series of dramatic
love stories created
especially for you
by world-acclaimed
authors.

If you've ever dreamed of...

- traveling to exotic places
- meeting new and interesting people
- thrilling to the excitement of love

then

Harlequin Presents...

are for you

The world's best-selling contemporary romance novels...
because Harlequin understands the way women the world over feel about love.

Harlequin Presents...

Six brand-new novels every month wherever paperback books are sold or through Harlequin Reader Service

In U.S.A.
MPO Box 707
Niagara Falls,
NY 14302

In Canada
649 Ontario Street
Stratford,
Ontario N5A 6W2

FREE!

**A hardcover Romance Treasury volume
containing 3 treasured works of romance
by 3 outstanding Harlequin authors...**

**...as your introduction to Harlequin's
Romance Treasury subscription plan!**

Romance Treasury

**...almost 600 pages of exciting romance reading
every month at the low cost of $5.97 a volume!**

A wonderful way to collect many of Harlequin's most beautiful love
stories, all originally published in the late '60s and early '70s.
Each value-packed volume, bound in a distinctive gold-embossed
leatherette case and wrapped in a colorfully illustrated dust jacket,
contains...
- 3 full-length novels by 3 world-famous authors of romance fiction
- a unique illustration for every novel
- the elegant touch of a delicate bound-in ribbon bookmark...
  and much, much more!

Romance Treasury

...for a library of romance you'll treasure forever!

Complete and mail today the FREE gift certificate and subscription
reservation on the following page.

Romance Treasury

An exciting opportunity to collect treasured works of romance! Almost 600 pages of exciting romance reading in each beautifully bound hardcover volume!

You may cancel your subscription whenever you wish! You don't have to buy any minimum number of volumes. Whenever you decide to stop your subscription just drop us a line and we'll cancel all further shipments.